Spieron Virche has served his coven as an enforcer for less than a decade when he's given the honorable task of helping a gargoyle elder. To his surprise, erasing the memory of the man threatening the other paranormal gives him an outsider's glimpse into a human who piques his interest—Albert Lindson. When Spieron is asked to lead the way to Albert, he's more than eager to do so. As soon as he meets the man, Spieron suspects the reason for his interest. He takes advantage of the man's shock at his son's unexpected arrival to taste the human's blood, and his world is turned upside down. Albert is Spieron's beloved, the other half of his soul. Too bad the aging mountain man is settled in his solitary life and expects to die alone within a few years. Can Spieron find a way not only to draw Albert back into the world but convince him that his life is far from over . . . in fact, could it be just beginning?

Blood of a Mountain Man
Copyright © 2019 Charlie Richards
ISBN: 978-1-4874-2480-0
Cover art by Angela Waters

Published by eXtasy Books Inc or
Devine Destinies, an imprint of eXtasy Books Inc

Look for us online at:
www.eXtasybooks.com or www.devinedestinies.com

Blood of a Mountain Man
A Paranormal's Love: Book Twenty-Six

By

Charlie Richards

DEDICATION

Happiness consists of living each day as if it were the first day of your honeymoon and the last day of your vacation.
~Leo Tolstoy

CHAPTER ONE

Spieron Virche leaned against the porch railing. Tipping his head back to rest on the end post, he allowed his thoughts to return to the stolen memories. As a vampire, he could enter a human's mind and manipulate their thoughts, which is exactly what he'd had to do to Baltus Lindson, the owner of the ranch where Spieron currently stayed as the guest of his son, Nicholas Lindson.

As Spieron enjoyed the sun on his face, a stolen memory pushed into his mind.

A young, brown-haired boy with a big grin on his face rode a large pony in a round pen. An adult male stood in the center, offering instruction. The man sported a big smile, and his eyes gleamed with pride.

Envy filled the older boy watching from the fence.

The recollection changed.

The brown-haired boy was older now, perhaps a young teenager. He galloped across the arena swinging a lariat and easily roped the calf. His horse skidded to a stop, popping the young cow off its feet. The rider swung from the saddle and ran to the struggling animal. He easily flipped the beast onto its back and successfully tied the calf's legs, then threw up his arms as he crowed with success.

"Great job, Albert," a man called out from where he was sitting on the fence holding a stopwatch — the foreman, Carl, the memory supplied. "You just beat your brother's time." The grinning man turned his attention on the watcher. "You gonna try again, Baltus?"

1

The watcher, Baltus, shook his head as anger simmered through him. "Naw, I got better stuff to do," he replied, twisting his lips into a smirk. "I have to study for school. I'm gonna be a lawyer like Dad. I'm gonna make this place some real money when I take over."

Carl frowned but didn't reply as Baltus rode his horse out of the arena, plans to buy the test the teacher used, stolen by a fellow student, already filling his mind.

Then Spieron focused on his favorite memory.

"Hey, you gonna help?"

Albert's shout drew Baltus's attention. He turned and spotted his younger brother hefting a bale of hay off the back of a wagon piled high with the stuff. Pivoting, Albert dropped the bale — which probably weighed in between ninety and one hundred pounds — onto the conveyor belt, sending the bale trundling up to the second story of the barn. Once at the top, Carl removed it, taking the bale into the depths of the barn.

Each move Albert made accentuated the muscles of his arms, chest, and abdominals, on clear display since he was shirtless in the hot Texas afternoon heat. Sweat gleamed on his body, and the black cowboy hat he wore shaded his face. It also darkened the five-o-clock shadow on Albert's face. His brother's jeans were damp with sweat, molding to his strong legs.

Baltus scoffed as he glanced down at his own clothes — dress slacks, polished boots, and a short-sleeved dress shirt. "Seriously?" Rolling his eyes, Baltus turned away from his brother and the hard work he was doing. "I'm headed off on a date with Katrina," he stated, casting a smirk his brother's way. He knew his little brother liked the beautiful teenager, too, but Baltus had every intention of winning her hand, first. She was rich, after all, and he —

Spieron ignored the rest of the memory in favor of re-calling Albert's sexy form as he'd been moving the hay. He wasn't certain what about the man drew him, and he knew the brother no longer looked like that, but Spieron found him fascinating. For some reason, Spieron desperately wanted to taste the human's full lips, and his desire to scent his blood almost felt like a physical hunger in his stomach.

Even feeling Baltus's negative emotions toward his brother didn't diminish Spieron's desire. As he focused on the bead of sweat that slid along his memory of Albert's cut abdominals, his mouth watered. He wanted to lick the sweat off the man, taste him, the desire causing Spieron's blood to heat and his prick to thicken.

"Are you ready to go?"

The deep voice of Elder Bodb cut through Spieron's thoughts. When he snapped his eyes open, he spotted the big male smirking down at him. His dark-brown eyes held a wicked gleam as he cut a pointed look at Spieron's groin.

"Or is there something on your mind that'll delay us?"

Even though the man before him appeared to be in his mid-to-late forties, Spieron knew better. As a vampire—a paranormal who lived upward of five hundred years—he appeared in his early thirties even though he'd walked the earth for one-hundred-thirty-seven years. Bodb, on the other hand, was a gargoyle, a paranormal that could live upward of two millennia. While Spieron wasn't certain of his exact age, he knew the male had crossed the thousand year mark long ago.

Spieron saw the smirk on Bodb's lips split into a wide grin, so he reined in his wandering thoughts. "No, of course not." There was no way he wanted to delay finding Albert Lindson. Spieron knew the human wouldn't look like the man in his stolen memories, and he wondered if his attraction would disappear once he found the man.

"Well, think of something else, then," Bodb ordered, his tone still laced with amusement. "Otherwise sitting in the truck for six hours is going to be hell."

Laughing, Spieron flipped the gargoyle off, then began leading the way down the porch steps. As he headed toward the truck, he pulled the keys out of his pocket. The vehicle was a newer model, king-cab diesel that Spieron had picked up the prior year.

Bodb's lover and mate, Nicholas, joined them after Spieron had climbed behind the wheel, and the pair sat in the back. The human looked nervous, swallowing hard enough to cause his Adam's apple to bob. As Spieron drove away from the ranch, he noticed the way Bodb took Nicholas's hand in an attempt to soothe him.

Nicholas smiled at his lover, the tension in his shoulders easing.

Spieron knew what bothered him.

Nicholas's father, Baltus Lindson, had discovered that Nicholas's marriage to Sandra was a farce, and he'd attempted to blackmail his son and his son's male lover—Bodb. What Baltus hadn't known was that Bodb was an elder of the gargoyle race. Using his contacts, he'd offered a favor to Spieron's leader—Master Adalric Bachmeier.

When his master had asked Spieron to go to Texas and aid the gargoyle elder, Spieron had considered it a great honor. After all, he'd only been an enforcer for the Esson coven for a little over a decade. Of course, the fact that Spieron was one of only a couple of enforcers that wasn't bonded probably had something to do with it.

And now, I'm obsessed with a memory taken from Baltus.

Spieron had a suspicion, but he hadn't shared it with either of the two men. He needed to scent Albert first.

No point in getting my hopes up even more than they already are.

Pushing the thought out of his mind, Spieron focused on the roads and the map in his head that he'd gleaned from Baltus's mind. The asshole had forced his younger brother out after they'd disagreed one too many times about Baltus's parenting methods. Baltus had revealed that he knew Nicholas was the result of an affair between Albert and Katrina and had threatened to disinherit him.

Albert had acquiesced, selling his share of the ranch to Baltus, and had left the ranch to live alone in the mountains.

Six hours later—and after a couple of pit stops for breaks—Spieron turned the truck off the highway and began making his way along narrower and narrower roads. They steadily climbed higher and deeper into the mountains. A glance in the rearview mirror revealed that Nicholas's tension was once again on the rise.

Not surprising, really, since they hadn't been able to call Albert to give him a heads up that they were coming. While Spieron knew the man had a satellite phone and had even been able to pull the number from Baltus's mind, every time they'd tried it, it had been turned off. Spieron assumed the only time Albert would turn it on was if he had an emergency.

The other option was that Albert had passed away, but Spieron hated to think that. It caused his gut to churn unpleasantly coupled with a burning need to hurt someone.

"Are you sure this is the area?" Nicholas asked quietly, leaning this way and that to peer out the windows in every direction.

Spieron gritted his teeth as he maneuvered around a pothole, then along a series of ruts. "Yes," he managed to respond. "Shit," he grumbled, wrenching the wheel to avoid a huge rock embedded in the road. "I'm pretty sure we're almost there."

Just as Spieron spoke the words, he rounded a bend, and the trees thinned to reveal a good-sized clearing. In the middle stood a small cabin with a few paving stones before the front door and smoke drifting from the chimney. To the right of the door stood a large stack of firewood.

To the right of the cabin was a lean-to that appeared to be

5

approximately ten-foot by twenty-foot and stood eight feet high. That structure was nearly filled to capacity with more firewood. There was a chicken coop to the left of the building, but the chickens were currently loose in the yard, pecking and scratching.

Spieron spotted another structure farther back as well as the edge of a fence behind the cabin, but he could only guess what that was attached to. As he parked, his attention was drawn to the front door, which was opening. Shutting off the engine, Spieron felt his breath catch in his throat.

A dark-haired man with a thick beard—both mixed with plenty of gray—stepped out of the cabin. Even though the guy rested a shotgun over the crook of his left elbow, his slightly grayed brows were furrowed, and his lips were drawn into a frown, Spieron admired his broad shoulders and thickly muscled limbs—accentuated by the faded jeans and rolled up sleeves of the flannel shirt he wore.

Even with the advanced age of the man, so different than the memories he'd been privy to, Spieron knew that this was Albert Lindson.

Need spiraled through Spieron—a desire to scent the man—so he pushed open his door.

"You're on private property, stranger," Albert stated. "You best get right back in that pick-up and get out of here."

Spieron opened his mouth, but any thought of a reply went right out of his head as the big, handsome man's scent tickled his senses. His stomach clenched, and his breath caught in his throat. He had to swallow hard so he didn't drool as his fangs ached with his desire to taste the wonderfully smelling man's blood.

"Uncle Albert!" Nicholas called from where he climbed out of the vehicle's opposite side's back seat.

"Nicholas?" Albert's dark brows shot up. "Is that you?"

Rounding the front of the truck, Nicholas nodded, a wide

grin on his face. "Yeah, it's me."

"How the hell did you find me, Nick?" Albert asked as he rested the shotgun against the woodpile. Then he opened his arms and grabbed Nicholas up in a bear hug, which Nicholas heartily returned.

"If I can deal with Nicholas being hugged by a strange man, then you can deal with Albert being hugged by my mate." Bodb's whispered words sounded in Spieron's ear, making him realize he was issuing a low growl, which he immediately cut off with a clear of his throat. Bodb chuckled softly as he asked, "Something you want to tell me?"

Spieron swallowed once more as he shoved his hands into his pockets. "I believe Albert may be my beloved," he murmured back.

"*May* be?"

Jerking a curt nod, Spieron admitted, "I need to taste his blood to be certain, but all the signs are there."

Bodb nodded, his eyes narrowing as he returned his focus to his mate. "Right. Well, that shouldn't be too hard."

Spieron's brows shot up as surprise filled him. "Too hard? How do you figure? I can't just sink my fangs into him."

Tipping his chin in the direction of the house, Bodb pointed out, "There's an axe right there. Maybe a stumble so he puts his hand on it? Or how about a mug shatters, and he cuts a finger." Shrugging, Bodb waggled his brows. "Hell, you could just grab him and lay one on him, scratching his tongue with your fang."

The more Bodb talked, the more Spieron's jaw sagged open. He began to shake his head, then paused. The last idea did have a little merit. The other's, not so much.

Spieron had no desire to hurt the man just to confirm that he was his beloved.

Even as Spieron thought about the best way to initiate a kiss with the man, another thought flitted through his mind.

Albert had had an affair to produce Nicholas. He wasn't certain if the big burly man would even be open to a relationship with him.

Damn it.

"What if he isn't gay?"

Bodb had the audacity to snort. "Even if he wasn't before, if he *is* your beloved, he's bisexual now."

"Huh." Spieron nodded. "True."

"Besides, if Albert is your beloved, it'll make it far easier for us to explain what happened to Baltus and how we found him." Bodb's expression turned serious as he added, "I know Nicholas hated the idea of lying to his . . . uncle."

Spieron nodded slowly, understanding since Nicholas always seemed like such a straight shooter. He already had to keep so many lies in his life due to being bonded with a paranormal. Hiding information when trying to reconnect with the man he'd always considered his uncle, but was actually his father, would be rough on the human.

With that knowledge in mind, when Nicholas finally turned and called for Bodb, Spieron approached, too. He stopped and stood back, watching as Nicholas took a deep breath, then introduced Bodb.

"Uncle Albert, this is my partner, Bodb."

Watching the way Albert's brows shot up, Spieron didn't even need to use his sense of smell to know that Nicholas had just shocked the shit out of the burly human.

CHAPTER TWO

Albert Lindson knew he gaped, but he couldn't seem to help himself. Not only had Nicholas shown up on his doorstep — *I didn't even know that he knew how to find me* — but he was introducing him to a partner . . . a male partner. While Albert had long accepted his own bisexuality, he'd never acted on it.

Is my son like me? Or is he gay?

Can't exactly ask that, since the man doesn't know his origins.

"Uncle Albert?" Nicholas touched his upper arm. "Is this gonna be a problem?"

Clearing his throat, Albert yanked his head out of his ass, mentally speaking, anyway. He quickly offered his son a wry smile. "Of course not. Just surprised." Albert turned his attention to Bodb and thrust out his hand. "Nice to meet you, Bodb."

As Bodb took his hand and offered a brief handshake, Albert discreetly checked the man out. He appeared to be in his mid-to-late forties, with thick gray hair which was pulled into a ponytail. Albert wasn't a small man by any means, standing at six-foot-three with a big, muscled body, but Bodb was even bigger than him, topping him by three inches.

Albert released Bodb as he glanced between them. "Well, the cabin ain't much, but ya'll are welcome to step in." As he picked up his shotgun, he wiped the sweat off his brow. "Although I ain't runnin' the generator right now, so it's still pretty hot."

"I bet it's cooler than at the ranch," Nicholas commented, grinning. "I can definitely feel a difference, being up in the mountains and all."

Nodding, Albert led the way inside. He felt the hairs on his nape as he crossed to the left and placed his shotgun on a rack he'd created for it using shed deer antlers that he'd found. As Albert turned, he indicated the room.

"You're welcome to sit wherever." Albert offered Nicholas a small smile. "It ain't much."

"This place is impressive for your location."

The smooth tenor belonged to the man Albert had been doing his best to ignore. Even though he hadn't been introduced, yet, it had been tough. Threatening the man with his shotgun had taken just about every bit of self-control he'd had.

In truth, Albert had wanted to invite the man in, then see if he had a shot at exploring every inch of the leanly muscled male.

Albert had never explored that side of himself. As he glanced from the stranger's handsome features, then to his son and back again, he wondered if he finally could. Of course, trying to figure out if another guy was interested . . . well, that was something he'd never had to do before.

Holding out his hand to the man, Albert offered, "I apologize for threatenin' ya." He grinned as he shrugged. "I get poachers up here occasionally, especially this time of year. Huntin' season just brings out the crazies."

"No apology necessary," the stranger all but purred as he stepped forward and took Albert's hand. "After all, I don't intend to apologize for this."

Albert opened his mouth to question the man, but he didn't get a chance. Instead, the man tightened his hold on his hand even as he stepped closer to him, right into Albert's personal space. He used his other hand to cradle Albert's nape, and with a gentle hold, the man urged Albert to dip his head down as he tipped his own back and pushed into him.

To Albert's shock, he felt the man seal his lips over his own. His heart skipped a beat as the stranger's warm, thin lips slid against Albert's own. The press and tease of the man's mouth moving over his own caused tingles to zip down his neck and across his chest.

When that sensation hit Albert's nipples, he gasped.

The other man took complete advantage, sweeping his tongue into Albert's mouth. The stranger teased along his tongue, encouraging him to join in the tongue-play. He mapped Albert's mouth, sliding along his gums, licking over his teeth, and swiping over his palate.

As a tremble worked through Albert, he brought his hands up and rested them on the guy's hips. His first instinct was to push away the brazen man, but the taste of the guy was quickly going to his head. Albert thought his flavor was the most exquisite combination of maleness and something sweet . . . like red licorice bites.

God, I love red licorice bites!

Wanting more of the man's amazing taste, Albert tightened his hold on his left hip. He moved his right hand to the stranger's strong jaw. Sliding it along the smooth bone-line, Albert used his hold to tip the other man's head, then took control of the kiss.

Albert sank his tongue into the other man's mouth, searching for more of that amazing flavor. Instantly, it burst across his tongue. Growling deep in his throat, Albert felt his aggression rising, and it was his turn to map the other man's mouth. He teased at the guy's tongue and lapped along his teeth.

To Albert's surprise, he came upon a tooth that was far sharper than he thought it should be. He slowed the kiss, sliding his appendage against it. For a second, Albert thought perhaps the man had a broken tooth.

Just that fast, Albert felt the lean man in his arms use his own tongue to push his against the tooth. A sharp pain shot through his tongue, and he nearly jerked away. Except, then the other man suckled his appendage lightly, creating a riot of sensations to flutter through Albert's gut.

Moaning roughly, Albert began to slide his arm around the guy's waist. He had every intention of pulling the man closer, flushing their bodies. Then he heard a low rough chuckle. Just that fast, Albert remembered where he was and who else was around.

Albert snapped his head up, breaking the kiss. Panting harshly, he stared at the man in his arms . . . and who was pressed tight against him. He couldn't remember when he'd pulled the man flush to his chest, but he sure liked it. Although, feeling a hard dick pushing into his upper thigh was definitely different.

"Well, hell," Nicholas commented, amusement in his tone. "It seems we have a hell of a lot to discuss." To Albert's relief, his son was staring at the guy he held, his lips curving into an amused smile as he lifted one eyebrow. "You got something to tell me, Spieron?"

Spieron grinned widely at Nicholas. "Oh, yes." In the next instant, he met Albert's gaze, showing off the fact that his canines were damn sharper than any he'd ever seen. "I was wondering why I found Baltus's memories of Albert so fascinating. Now I know." As Albert stared down at him, Spieron slid his thumb over the hair on his top lip. "Albert is my beloved."

"Congratulations," Bodb immediately responded.

Nicholas, however, his brows shot up, and he cocked his head. "Damn. Really?" A second later, his eyes twinkled as he stated, "Cool."

Their responses confused Albert just as much as his odd

uninhibited display did. Realizing he still held the stranger—Spieron—he lifted his hands and took a step backward. He didn't know if he was upset or pleased that Spieron let him go without a fight.

"Hey, do you have any beer here?"

Nicholas's question drew Albert's attention. His mind reeled, and he was having a hard time focusing.

"Uh . . . beer?"

"I'll get what we brought from the truck," Spieron offered as he took another step away from Albert. "I think Albert may need a minute to get his brain back online." His lips curved into a lascivious smile even as his eyes narrowed into a heated gaze. "A minute now would be good, since he's going to be processing a lot of information this evening."

Albert furrowed his brows as confusion filled him. He rubbed the back of his neck as he watched Spieron leave the cabin. Once the door was closed, he turned his attention to Nicholas.

"S-Son? What's going on?"

Albert stood stock-still, tension thrumming through him . . . as was arousal. His dick was hard enough to pound nails. Trying to engage his brain, Albert watched as Nicholas approached him. When the man everyone knew as his nephew touched his arm, Albert flinched.

"A lot has happened since you left," Nicholas stated as he wrapped his right arm around Albert's waist. He gripped his forearm with his left hand and began guiding him to the small table near the back of the cabin. "So many secrets revealed," Nicholas continued softly. "Mine, yours, Baltus's." With his lips curving into a wry smile, he added, "Even Bodb's and Spieron's. We really do have a lot to discuss."

"Some secrets are dangerous, Nicholas," Albert whispered as he settled onto one of the wooden chairs at the round table. Meeting Nicholas's gaze as his son settled next to him, he added, "To a great many people."

Nicholas's smile held a wealth of understanding. "Never have truer words been spoken." Resting his forearms on the table, he held Albert's gaze. "And I hope you'll remember that as we talk."

Even as Albert nodded, he couldn't help feeling a fissure of unease as he took in Nicholas's serious expression. So rarely had he seen such a look on the man, since normally he was so laid-back. Clearing his throat, Albert returned his son's gaze with a level look of his own.

"Very well. What secrets must we discuss today?"

Sighing, Nicholas glanced over at Bodb, who responded by joining them at the table. Bodb took Nicholas's hand, twining their fingers, obviously offering his support.

The look of love that passed between the pair caused Albert's heart to skip a beat. He couldn't ever remember anyone peering at him in such a way. While he didn't want to feel envy at Nicholas's good fortune, it was damn tough to squelch.

Once Nicholas returned his focus to Albert, his smile turned a little wan. "How about we start at the beginning? Hmm?"

Albert cocked his head, uncertain what Nicholas meant. He stayed silent, waiting.

Nicholas cleared his throat, then said almost on a whisper, "My beginning, anyway." With his eyes furrowing, hinting some internal hurt, he slipped his tongue out, licking the bottom one. After a sharp nod—maybe he'd been giving himself an internal pep talk—for Nicholas softly stated, "You're not my uncle. You're my father."

Straightening in his seat, Albert tensed. He clenched his hands into fists on the table. His brain stalled.

Lifting his hand, palm out, Nicholas continued in a firm, quiet voice. "I know you had an affair with Mom. I can even guess as to why everyone hid the fact." His mouth twisted into a scowl, and his gaze lowered to where he held hands with Bodb. "Mom didn't want to lose her rich and comfortable lifestyle through divorce. Dad, uh"—Nicholas paused an instant while shaking his head—"Uncle Baltus wanted to save face. Not good for business for it to be known his new wife was already stepping out on him. Especially with his brother." Nicholas finally lifted his head and focused on Albert. "I just can't figure out your motives . . . Dad."

Albert sucked in a deep breath, then let it out on a long sigh. "God," he whispered. "It was so very long ago. I—"

Shit.

How could he explain that the whole sordid affair was done out of spite?

Hell, on both sides.

"Oh, Nicholas, that's an easy question," Spieron stated, announcing that he'd return to the cabin. He carried several plastic bags in each hand as he crossed the small cabin. His thin lips were curved into a mild smile, and his aristocratic features sported a look that Albert couldn't quite decipher.

Pain, maybe? But why?

As Spieron placed the bags on the counter, Nicholas asked, "What are you talking about."

Spieron pulled out a six-pack of beer and crossed to the table. After placing the cardboard carrier on the scarred surface, he met Nicholas's gaze. "It's the oldest story in the book, my friend. Two brothers. One woman. Trouble." Nicholas straightened while cocking his head. Spieron turned and peered into Albert's eyes. "You both wanted her at one point, didn't you? And after everything was said and done, Baltus won, and you were . . . jealous?"

Albert gaped. Shock flooded him.

How could this man know all that?

As Albert watched, Spieron shifted his focus to the beer. His expression turned shuttered as he began pulling out beer bottles, opening them, and placing one in front of everyone. Once done with that, Spieron settled in the fourth and final chair, then wrapped his hands around his beer.

Finally, Albert pegged Spieron's expression.

Jealous. The man is jealous.

Considering the kiss they'd shared, Albert knew he shouldn't be surprised. He was, though—at least, a little bit. They'd just met after all.

"Dad?"

Hearing Nicholas call him that caused Albert's breath to catch in his chest. He swallowed hard, then forced himself to meet his son's gaze. "You have no idea how many times I wished for you to call me that."

Nicholas offered him a tremulous smile. He was obviously having just as tough a time dealing with Spieron's bald comments as Albert was with Nicholas's revelation. His son reached across the table with his free hand and gripped Albert's.

"Is that true? You, uh"—Nicholas paused to clear his throat—"you wanted Mom, so—" He paused, his words stalling.

"I didn't force your mother," Albert quickly offered, squeezing Nicholas's hand so his focus returned to his own. Seeing his son's questioning look, he admitted, "She came to me. Your father, uh—" He winced.

Old habits and so forth.

Scoffing, Nicholas muttered, "I still slip, too."

"So, uh, you know how Baltus yells when he wants to make a point." Albert waited a few seconds, then saw Nicholas nod. "Your mother was on the receiving end of a particularly vicious rant, so she came crying to me. I—" Issuing a deep sigh, Albert shook his head. "She wanted to be held, and I was handy. Then she revealed that she'd found out that I had liked her, too, but Baltus had asked her out on a date first, bein' older, and I missed my shot."

Releasing Nicholas's hand, he grabbed for his beer. With his other hand, he rubbed the back of his neck as he thought just how much to explain. As he decided, Albert took a deep swallow of beer.

"Except you didn't miss your shot entirely." It was Spieron who spoke, his voice soft and full of understanding. He reached out and rested his long, slender fingers over Nicholas's wrist. "She came onto you, and you took what she offered."

Albert met Spieron's gaze and offered a single nod. "Yeah. And after it was done, said we couldn't do it again." Lowering his gaze to the table, he mumbled, "But we did. Until about two months later when a condom broke, and she ended up pregnant."

Shame flooded Albert, but he forced himself to meet Nicholas's gaze. "I know we shouldn'ta done what we did, but I'll never regret it, because it gave me you . . . even if I couldn't claim ya as mine."

Nicholas's eyes gleamed, and he blinked quickly even as he smiled back at him. "Believe it or not, I do understand." He cast a swift smile Bodb's way, then revealed, "Sometimes you have to make tough choices. You see . . . I'm actually married to a woman. Her name's Sandra."

For the second time in less than an hour, Albert felt as if he'd been hit upside the head with a two-by-four.

"Y-You're—" He glanced between a calm-looking Bodb and his flush-faced son. "What?"

CHAPTER THREE

Seeing the shock mixed with confusion flash across Albert's features, Spieron cleared his throat. He rubbed his thumb over the pulse point in Albert's wrist, doing his best to soothe. Catching his beloved's eye, he offered an encouraging smile.

Then he turned his gaze on Nicholas. "Perhaps you should explain that," he said with a smile. "Your comment did sound sort of cryptic."

Nicholas chuckled softly as he nodded. "Yeah. Sorry about that . . . Dad."

When Albert heard that simple word, his face lit up.

That look on Albert's face caused Spieron's heart rate to spike in his veins. His hand on his beloved's wrist twitched, and he enjoyed the feel of the human's hair on his arm as it slid beneath the pads of his fingers. It also drew Albert's attention to the fact that they still touched.

Spieron could see the questions filling Albert's eyes, so he winked, then used his free hand to point at Nicholas. As much as he wanted to explain about their bond right away, he knew Nicholas had to come first. His beloved needed that connection. It would help in the long run.

Albert's eyes narrowed as he turned his attention back to Nicholas. Even as his son opened his mouth to begin explaining, Albert blurted out, "Has something happened to Baltus?"

Nicholas hesitated, then nodded. "Yeah. Uh . . . that's part of the story." He lifted his free hand, clearly asking for patience. "Um ... so—" Nicholas heaved a sigh, obviously struggling.

"Start at the beginning, love," Bodb urged softly, lifting their twined hands and pressing a kiss to Nicholas's knuckles. His brown eyes twinkle as he added, "Considering the lip-lock Albert shared with Spieron as well as his acceptance of us, I'm pretty sure he'll understand."

After blowing out a deep breath, Nicholas nodded. He curved his lips into a pained smile, then launched into his explanation.

Spieron remained quiet, listening. He'd heard bits and pieces of the issues Nicholas had had with Baltus—the man he'd always thought was his father. When Spieron had delved into Albert's brother's mind, he'd learned differently.

Talk about a shock to Nicholas.

"So, you married Sandra to be her beard?" Albert stated, rubbing his own beard—the physical one—thoughtfully. After Nicholas grunted in assent, Albert peered at Bodb. "And you and Maggie were okay with it?" he asked, referring to Sandra's partner of three years.

Bodb smiled, glancing Nicholas's way with love shining in his dark eyes. "I'd do just about anything for Nicholas," he admitted, meeting Albert's gaze. His expression turned serious. "I met Nicholas a couple of weeks before his wedding."

Albert jumped on that. "You've only known each other for a couple of weeks?" Leaning forward, he wrapped both his hands around his beer bottle, pulling away from Spieron. "You started seeing each other even though you knew Nicholas was marrying Sandra?"

Spieron could see the agitation thrumming through Albert, but he wasn't entirely certain from where it stemmed.

"Yes," Bodb answered bluntly. "Like I said. I'd do just about anything for Nicholas." He turned his attention to Spieron. "You ready for me to open the can of worms?"

Humming, Spieron nodded once. "Better sooner rather than later," he stated with a wide grin, knowing he showed off his fangs. Spieron knew Albert had seen them, too, considering the way his bearded lips parted and his thick brows shot up. As he licked his tongue over his left fang, he winked at Albert. "And, yes, these are real, handsome."

"What the hell?"

Nicholas lifted both hands, pulling away from Bodb. "Okay, so . . . this is gonna sound a little . . . unbelievable, but please let us get it all out. Okay?"

"Ooookay." Albert's eyes narrowed. "But you still haven't explained what happened to Baltus."

"Right, right." Nicholas shifted in his seat. His brows were furrowed, and he was bobbing his head in an absent manner. "Well, uh, fa—um, Baltus." After rolling his eyes, he twisted his lips into a wry smile. "It's definitely taking some getting used to."

Albert's whisker-covered lips twitched, and his brown eyes took on a soft gleam.

Spieron's chest thudded at that expression, and he hoped to someday have the look of affection aimed at him.

Nicholas cleared his throat, then continued. "So, Baltus got it in his head that he wanted to gain entrance to what his research said was an exclusive nudist colony." When Albert's eyebrows shot up and he scoffed, Nicholas snorted as he nodded. "Yeah, not something you'd think he'd be interested in, but he'd heard that a lot of wealthy people attended there." Nicholas shook his head, frowning. "Not surprising, Baltus wanted to talk business with the people, which probably would have ostracized him pretty fast anyway."

"A nudist colony?" Albert lifted his beer to his lips and took a sip. "I sure wouldn't want to see that."

As Spieron mentally agreed, Nicholas nodded. "Anyway, Night Wingers, Inc. isn't really a nudist colony. That's just the cover they use" — he waved his hand as he shook his head — "more on that in a sec. So, Baltus was denied entrance, but you know how he is when he gets his mind set on something."

Albert actually growled low in his throat as he nodded once and crossed his arms over his chest.

Hearing that sound made by the sexy, rugged man, Spieron felt his blood heat in his veins. His hard dick twitched. He reached down and adjusted himself, attempting to find a more comfortable position for his swollen shaft.

The move drew Albert's attention, and his eyes widened a little. His lips parted, and if Spieron didn't miss his guess, he spotted a faint glow staining Albert's cheeks beneath his salt and pepper beard. Gritting his teeth, Spieron just stopped himself from grabbing the man.

Nicholas continuing to speak helped Spieron keep his control, too.

It also drew Albert's attention back to the other man.

Too bad.

Patience, damn it! We'll have centuries together.

"Baltus realized that my wedding to Sandra was a sham, and since I met Bodb while we were in Durango, he thought Bodb was someone important at Night Wingers." Nicholas leaned into Bodb's touch when the big man slung his arm around the back of Nicholas's chair and slid his fingertips up and down his upper arm. The move seemed to bolster Nicholas's courage, for he charged ahead, saying, "When Baltus blackmailed us, demanding that Bodb give him entrance to Night Wingers as well as stock in the company, otherwise he'd reveal to Sandra's father the truth of my relationship with her, Bodb brought in Spieron."

Nicholas waved Spieron's way, which pulled Albert's attention back to him, and he smiled at his beloved.

Nicholas kept talking. "Like I said, Night Wingers isn't actually a nudist colony. It's actually a gargoyle clutch."

Those words had Albert snapping his gaze back to Nicholas, and Spieron watched his human closely, wondering how he would handle the upcoming revelations.

Spieron held up his hand. "I'm sorry, did you just say *gargoyle clutch?*"

"Yes, I did," Nicholas replied, his tone serious. "I told you it might sound odd." He shrugged, grinning. "Gargoyles, well, paranormals in general, I suppose, they don't appreciate threats to their secrecy, which Baltus was, so"—once again, Nicholas pointed at Spieron—"Bodb asked for a favor from a vampire coven in New Mexico, and the master there sent Spieron. Spieron altered Baltus's mind, making him forget, um . . . just about everything."

Gaping, Albert glanced around at everyone. His focus finally settled on Spieron . . . or more accurately, on his mouth. It didn't take a genius to figure out what Albert was thinking about.

Spieron once again grinned, allowing the heat of his desire to fill him, causing his eyes to haze. The room around him took on a reddish hue, and he knew his irises would appear red to others. Resting his hand on the table, Spieron extended his three-inch claws and tapped them on the tabletop a few times.

Albert gasped and jumped from his seat, causing it to tumble backward. His beloved nearly toppled himself, throwing out his arm to catch himself on the wall to the left.

The man's shout and response caused Spieron to immediately revert back to normal.

"Wh-Wh-What?" Albert stuttered, waving his pointer finger in Spieron's direction.

"That might not have been the best way," Bodb commented dryly as Nicholas rose to his feet and crossed to his father.

Spieron grimaced even as he nodded. Meeting the gargoyle's amused gaze, he admitted, "I thought *seeing is believing* coupled with *the rip off the bandage approach* would be best." Returning his focus to Albert, Spieron slowly rose from his seat with his hands lifted in placation. He saw the way Nicholas had one hand resting on Albert's shoulder, but Spieron felt a wash of pleasure that his beloved was still focused on him. "My apologies for springing that on you, Albert. I should have warned you."

"Uncle Albert. Father. *Please.* Spieron would never hurt you." Nicholas peered Spieron's way, lifting a brow. "Right?"

"Right," Spieron confirmed. "I would never hurt you. You're my beloved." He rested his right hand on his chest and offered his human a reassuring smile. "You're the other half of my soul, Albert. I will do anything and everything in my power to keep you safe and happy." Just thinking about all the things he wanted to do to make his beloved *happy*, Spieron let out a quiet moan. "It would be my honor."

Albert finally tore his focus away from Spieron so he could peer at Nicholas. "Nick? What the hell is going on?"

Nicholas heaved a deep sigh as he encouraged him back toward his chair. Spieron quickly turned the chair upright again. Seeing the way Albert eyed him warily, he bit back a curse at his stupidity.

"So, right. Like I said. Spieron is a vampire," Nicholas repeated, his tone gentle. "And Bodb is a gargoyle. They're two species of paranormals. There are others out there, too, but we don't have to get into that right now."

Albert settled back on his chair, but his back remained stiff, his muscles tense. After grabbing his beer, he lifted it to his lips. He gulped the rest of it, then placed the empty back on the table.

Spieron grabbed another from the carton, popped the top off, and set it in front of Albert. Although his expression remained wary, Albert still nodded his thanks.

"So, a gargoyle." Albert's voice sounded a little rusty, proving he was struggling to process. He swept his gaze over Bodb. "Do you have claws, too?"

"I have more than that," Bodb told him. "Wings, claws, thicker hide." He spread his arms wide, indicating himself. "And my actual skin color is dark purple, but I'm not going to show you all that right now."

"You're not?" Albert cocked his head. "Why?"

Bodb shook his head. "Because one freak out is enough, don't you think?" Then he leaned forward, settling his forearms on the table. "Back to explanations. Your son was trying to do a fine thing by agreeing to marry Sandra, even if it seems a little odd to those on the outside looking in." Bodb cast a warm smile Nicholas's way before refocusing on Albert. "You asked why I was okay with it, and I told you I would do anything for Nicholas. That's true, too, and besides, it's only for a decade or so, and with the prospect of living centuries together, that's just a drop in the bucket of our time together."

Spieron watched as Albert's thick eyebrows drew together. "Centuries?" his beloved asked. He focused on Spieron. "You live for centuries?"

Nodding, Spieron rested his left arm on the table, leaning closer to Albert. The draw of sitting beside his beloved was just too great. His instincts screamed at him to soothe the man, to take him somewhere where he could help him relax.

"A vampire can live upward of five hundred years," Spieron claimed, keeping his voice as soft and relaxed as he could. "Gargoyles are much longer lived, living somewhere around two thousand years."

Seeing Albert gape, Spieron paused, wondering if there would be a question in there somewhere.

There was.

Albert focused on Nicholas. "Why did he say you would have centuries together?"

Spieron smiled. His beloved caught on quick.

"Because one of the side effects of bonding is that my life-thread is now intertwined with Bodb's," Nicholas explained slowly. His smile took on a hint of deep-seated pleasure when he flashed a grin Bodb's way. "I will live as long as he does. Together with my mate." Then he refocused on Albert. "There are other side effects, too. Better health and strength. Harder to break bones or get sick. Having a partner who is completely, one hundred percent devoted to you."

When disbelief crossed Albert's features, Spieron touched his wrist lightly. Even though his beloved tensed, he didn't pull away. "Once a paranormal bonds with his Fate-given beloved, he can't even get it up for another." His beloved gaped, his brows shooting up, and Spieron chuckled. "It's just the way we're wired." Then his eyes narrowed, and he couldn't bite back his low growl. "And if another touches our other half, it's practically a death sentence."

"Why are you telling me this?" Albert finally blurted out. "Are you intending to wipe my mind like you did my brother's?"

"No," Spieron replied, holding Albert's gaze steadily. "We're telling you all this because *you* are *my* beloved, my other half." Rubbing Albert's wrist lightly with his finger-tips, massaging the dusting of hair there, Spieron continued, "I have been searching for you for over a hundred years, Albert."

CHAPTER FOUR

Albert slid the tines of the pitchfork beneath the soiled bedding. Lifting it, he took a few steps to the left and plopped the dirty straw, hay, and manure into the nearby wheelbarrow. Then he turned and repeated the procedure.

Losing himself in the repetitive exercise, Albert allowed the action to shut down his mind. That worked for about fifteen minutes until he'd finished cleaning the two stalls in his small barn. After dumping the manure in the pile where he worked it into compost for his garden, Albert rested his hands on his hips and stared at his two horses grazing amidst the trees.

With that chore done, Albert's mind immediately shifted to the shitload of information that had been dumped on him.

My son knows the truth about our relationship. Baltus has been removed from head of the family by a vampire because he threatened the safety of gargoyles. Oh, and said vampire wants to bond with me and drink my blood for centuries.

Albert shook his head, grabbed the handles of the wheelbarrow, and headed back to the barn. Pausing at the wall, he lifted the handles and flipped the barrow up to lean on the side of the barn. Grabbing the handkerchief out of his back pocket, he wiped it over his brow as he headed toward the woodpile.

As he pulled his axe from his splitting stump, he had to acknowledge that *that* was the part he was having the hardest time with. He was happy to finally be able to acknowledge his son, even if it was only in private. He was even happy that Nicholas had found love . . . even if it was with a man who thought he was a gargoyle.

Could that actually be a real thing?

Grabbing a log, Albert set it on its end on the stump. He swung his axe, using a little arm heft mixed with the momentum of the swing to slice the log. Picking up one of the halves, he returned it to the stump, balancing it on its end.

Albert concentrated on the simple routine of splitting logs into usable sizes until his shoulders screamed, his arms ached, and sweat caused his flannel shirt to stick to his torso. While he'd noticed Nicholas join him and begin stacking the wood he'd split, he didn't stop his work. Instead, Albert just flashed his son a smile and kept on going.

Finally, Albert slammed the axe head back into the stump. He lifted his arms over his head and groaned as he stretched his tired muscles. Twisting and turning, working out the kinks, Albert rested a side-eyed glance on Nicholas and watched him place the last of the wood on his woodpile.

"I know you asked for time, but watching you split wood makes me think it's gonna be tough to talk you into returning to the ranch."

Albert instantly lowered his arms and rested his hands on his hips. Then he grimaced and grabbed his bandana again. Wiping it over his forehead and eyes, down his beard, and across his neck, Albert let out a deep sigh.

"Damn sweat in my eyes stings like a bitch," Albert grumbled. Then he met Nicholas's gaze. "I'm not sure I have a place there, anymore, Nick. You run the place now, I hear." Even as he watched his son lift a hand and open his mouth, Albert added, "Not sure what I'd do there."

"That's a bullshit answer, and we both know it."

Hearing the growled words, Albert gaped at Nicholas. He couldn't ever remember seeing his son offer that response. Cocking his head, he lifted one eyebrow.

"What the hell do you mean by that?"

"Come on, Uncle Albert." Nicholas paused and shook his head. "Dad. That's an excuse. We both got railroaded by Uncle Baltus. Mitch, too. The only one who's happy is Vernon, and that's because he's following in Baltus's asshole footsteps." Stepping close, Nicholas placed his hand on Albert's shoulder and squeezed lightly. "I've missed you. Come home."

Albert couldn't hold Nicholas's gaze. Peering around, he took in his mountain retreat. He'd been left the cabin by their father, since he was the one who'd enjoyed going hunting with the man. Their father had been supportive of Baltus, too, and encouraged his ideas on how to expand the family empire.

Their father had been great like that. Too bad the only lessons Baltus seemed to learn from their dad had been how to pit sons against each other.

Or maybe it was the fact that Baltus had known from the beginning that Nicholas wasn't his own.

Albert rested his hand over Nicholas's and offered the man a smile. "You have no idea how proud I am of you."

"I had a fantastic teacher," Nicholas told him with a slight smile. "Now tell me the real reason you won't entertain the idea of coming home." Glancing around, he indicated the area. "I get that this is paradise, but it's hard work. And you're alone. What if something happens to you? How would you—" Nicholas froze for several seconds, then slowly turned his head away from the view and focused on Albert. "That was your plan, wasn't it?"

Feeling the blood rush to his face, Albert did his best to hold Nicholas's gaze. He couldn't. Sighing deeply, he swept his gaze over the area, taking in his one-bedroom cabin, his firewood shed, the small workshop lean-to, the chickens and their coop, and his horses' cozy barn and acres of paddock that disappeared amidst the trees.

When Albert had moved out there almost five years before, shortly after Mitch had up and left in the night just after high school, there had only been the cabin and firewood structure. He had built everything else. Between that, cutting firewood, and farming, hunting, and trapping for his food, Albert had stayed damn busy.

During that time, Albert had only gone to town two or three times a year and always during the summer. In the winter, his road was damn near impassable. Then every spring he spent a good week clearing downed trees and shoveling in ruts, that way he could head to town to stock up on everything he'd run out of during the winter.

"Dad?"

Albert pulled his focus from the beautiful if remote area he'd lived in for so long. Meeting Nicholas's gaze, he murmured, "I did expect to die here." He curved his lips into a wry smile. "And I can't think of a better place in which to end my days."

A low warning growl revealed they weren't alone.

Spinning, Albert pulled away from Nicholas and stepped to the left to place himself between his son and the danger. His jaw sagged open when he realized it wasn't a wild animal that had wandered too close. Instead, Spieron stood there . . . and his expression appeared thunderous.

"Spieron?" Albert asked warily. He kept his arms loose at his sides and did his best not to make any sudden movements. "Spieron? Is something wrong?"

How the hell was he supposed to know what kinds of things would set off a vampire?

"You speak of dying so cavalierly, Albert," Spieron snarled, his green eyes narrowed accusingly. "Why when I've just met you?"

"Well, I'm fifty-eight years old," Albert began slowly, trying to understand the question. "I live out in the woods, and it's dangerous. I —"

"Think carefully," Nicholas whispered, touching his side in warning. "You're talking about dying to a man whose entire purpose in life is to keep you alive, happy, and healthy."

After that, Nicholas slipped around him and strode away from them both. Before Albert could think up a response, his son called over his shoulder, "And you're his beloved. He'd never hurt you."

Albert took a deep breath, then let it out slowly. He met Spieron's narrow-eyed gaze. While his mind scrambled, he did his best to control the speed of his pulse even as he felt his heart threaten to pound out of his chest.

"You're upset because I speak of death, but that's just another facet of life, Spieron," Albert pointed out carefully. "I was forced out here by my brother, or he would disinherit my son." Holding the vampire's gaze, he stated calmly, "While I built myself a comfortable life out here, yes, I fully expected to die here."

Spieron growled again, and his eyes flashed red.

Clenching his jaw, Albert forced himself to remember Nicholas's words. The vampire wouldn't hurt him. He watched Spieron clench and unclench his hands before lifting one to rub the back of his neck.

In the next instant, Spieron's eyes returned to normal. His expression eased somewhat. At least, the rage disappeared. In its place became a steely resolve, his eyes narrowing as he swept his gaze over Albert over and over. At the same time, he stepped closer.

"You are my beloved," Spieron claimed once again. "I get that you needed time, that you needed to step away so you can process all the shit we dumped on you." Resting his hands on Albert's shoulders, he massaged lightly with his fingertips. "But as Nicholas said, I wish only to keep you safe, happy, and healthy." Spieron grinned suddenly, his eyes glittering. "Also, well-sexed." His focus slipped to Albert's groin, then back to his face. "Very, *very* well-sexed."

Albert sucked in a shocked gasp. Absently, he rubbed his hand over his stomach. Working hard every day had kept him in fantastic shape for his age, but he still no longer had a six-pack. From the hungry look in Spieron's eyes, that certainly didn't seem to matter to the man — vampire.

That'll take some getting used to.

"You talk about sex," Albert slowly mused, trying to put into words the thoughts he'd been having while doing chores and allowing his mind to drift. "But really isn't all you need is my blood?"

Spieron scoffed softly even as he shook his head. After a glance over his shoulder — Albert followed his gaze and spotted Nicholas peering out the window at them, held in the arms of his lover — the sexy auburn-haired man slid his arm around Albert's waist. With deceptive strength, Spieron turned him and urged him to start walking toward a bench Albert had placed near his workshop.

Some things — like cleaning tack — were just easier to do while sitting down . . . especially after a hard day of running his trap line or processing a wild hog he'd managed to hunt.

"There's something about vampires that is unique to paranormals," Spieron told him as they both settled on the wooden bench carved out of a log. His voice was deceptively quiet, and he took Albert's hand. "Unlike a shifter, who with the help of his pack, could possibly survive if his mate walked away, I cannot do that. Now that I've found you and tasted your blood, I no longer have the ability to drink from others." Spieron grimaced even as he lifted a hand and made a so-so gesture. "I suppose it's possible I could live my life on bagged blood, but it would be a half-life . . . a torturous existence . . . especially knowing that my beloved is out there, and I'm not by his side.

"So, yes, I require your blood to live, and now that I've tasted yours, seen you, kissed you, touched you . . ." Spieron reached out and scraped his fingertips along Albert's beard-ed cheek, then down the extra crinkly hair beneath. "I don't wish to spend the rest of my life without you." Spieron probably read the disbelief in his expression, even as he fought back a shiver at the feel of the man's touch. "I wish to get to know you, to figure out a way to share our lives." Lifting his hand and indicating the area, he added, "If that means spending the next couple of decades here in the woods, living off the land, until you're ready to join your son on his ranch, then that's what we'll do."

"I . . . I . . ." Albert cocked his head. He rubbed his hands over his face as he tried to process Spieron's words.

Just what the fuck am I supposed to say to that?

Finally, the question came, and Albert lowered his hands so he could meet the vampire's gaze. "Are you saying that you'd drop everything and live here on the mountain with me . . . just so you could drink my blood?"

Spieron's lips curved, and his eyes gleamed with amusement. "No, Albert. That's not what I'm saying."

"Then what?"

"I'm *saying* that I would drop everything and live here on the mountain with you because I want to make you happy." Spieron shrugged as he swept his gaze around the area. "You're right. This is a gorgeous place to stay." He winked before adding, "Just don't think I'm going to give up a few of the niceties. We'll definitely be making runs into town more often than you had." Spieron's expression heated once more. "You should consider, however, the more time we spend together, the harder it will be to resist our desire to bond . . . especially since I will find a pleasurable way to drink from you at least every other week."

"Wait. Pleasurable way to—" Albert couldn't help but scowl in disbelief at that. "Getting bitten is supposed to feel good?"

Spieron actually chuckled as he shook his head. "Not *sup-*

posed to, my beloved. It *does*. In fact"—turning on the bench seat to face Albert, he rested his left hand on Albert's thigh and massaged his taut muscle, making it jump—"you will enjoy it so much that you will orgasm from it." Spieron smirked. "I won't even have to touch you."

Except, brazen as you please, Spieron did touch Albert. It was just his fingertips, and the ghosting caress was feather-light against his trapped erection. Spieron did this once, twice, then returned his hand to Albert's thigh and squeezed once more.

"The pleasure we'll derive from the intimate act of me drinking your blood . . . it will make you crave more," Spieron warned. "You'll love it and begin to need us to complete our bond just as I need it, too." Skimming his fingers up Albert's thigh, Spieron lifted his hand to his chest, rubbing over his pectorals. "It's the way of paranormals." He grinned, showing off those oh-so-pointed canines—fangs. "Fate loves to get her way, and I've waited for you for over one hundred years. I can wait for another week . . . month . . . year. However long it takes to win your trust and understanding."

Albert wanted to cry bullshit, but from the expression on Spieron's face, he just knew the vampire believed what he was saying.

That didn't stop him from deciding he needed to test the vampire. After all, trust was a tricky thing where he came from. That was why he'd chosen to live alone all these years.

"How long do I have to decide?"

Spieron smiled, his tension relaxing. "As long as I'm allowed to be by your side so I can keep you safe . . . however long you need."

CHAPTER FIVE

Nicholas and Bodb stayed for the rest of the week. During that time, Spieron kept his advances subtle, since there was little privacy in the one-bedroom cabin. That didn't mean he didn't touch his man, because he did . . . light strokes down his back, across his ass, and along his arm . . . or some other part of his body.

Plus, Spieron took every opportunity he could to twine their fingers and hold his hand, even if for just a few seconds.

Spieron's goal — to get Albert used to his touch.

During the days, Spieron took a step back and watched as Albert reconnected with Nicholas. They checked his mountain man's trap line and went scouting together for hog tracks. Spieron stayed at the cabin with Bodb and discussed possible repercussions to what they'd done to Baltus.

Wiping a human's mind and putting him in a hospital — rather than killing him — always had the propensity for unforeseen issues. However, Bodb had promised not to simply kill the man, permanently removing the issue. Spieron had followed orders.

With Spieron sticking around, he had to be ready. There was a possibility the middle son, or a lawyer, could cause issues with Nicholas. They hadn't known enough about Baltus's dealings when Spieron had cleared his memory, and he took the quiet time to share everything he'd gleaned from the bastard's mind, giving Bodb the chance to start making plans.

At one point, Spieron drove into town to seek out a new cell phone provider. The cabin wasn't *that* remote, and he surmised that Albert used a satellite phone because he didn't actually want to be contacted by anyone. His beloved's family ties were so twisted, Spieron couldn't blame him.

Spieron, however, he intended to stay in touch with his coven, even if he had no idea how long it would be before he could return.

With his new phone in hand, Spieron relaxed in a chair outside the cabin and called home.

"Who is this?"

Spieron smiled upon hearing Master Adalric's cool tones. The sharp question didn't surprise him. He had called his master's direct line from a strange number, after all.

"Master Adalric, this is Spieron," he said, identifying himself.

"Ah, Spieron." Adalric's voice immediately warmed. "How are you? Have you completed your mission for Elder Bodb? When should we expect you home?"

Hearing Adalric's stream of questions caused Spieron's chest to warm. The man was a good master vampire, making every effort to keep up with the lives of those under his command. Adalric was a far cry better than the master of Spieron's birth coven.

Spieron dismissed the thought as he answered Adalric. "I'm doing well, Master. And yes and no."

"Well, that's not very informative, Enforcer Spieron," Adalric responded dryly. "How about a report."

Unable to help himself, Spieron chuckled. "Yes, I finished the assignment for Elder Bodb," he revealed. "But it brought up some unexpected consequences."

Adalric scoffed softly. "Doesn't it always? Okay. What's going on? Do you need assistance?"

"Not at this time, but I need permission to stay out here

for the foreseeable future." Grinning widely, Spieron told his master, "I met my beloved, but he needs some wooing."

"Congratulations, Spieron," Adalric instantly replied. "Finding one's beloved is cause for celebration. I take it he's human? I suppose I shouldn't assume he's a male, just because mine is," Adalric finished on a low chuckle.

"True, but yes, he's male. His name is Albert Lindson."

"Lindson? Relative?"

Spieron nodded even though he knew Master Adalric couldn't see it. "He is. When I searched Baltus's mind before clearing it, I discovered that Albert was living in the mountains . . . and that he's also Nicholas's father."

"Wait," Adalric cut in. "I thought that was Baltus."

"Evidently, there was an affair." While he struggled not to, Spieron couldn't quite keep the growl out of his voice. No vampire wanted to think of their beloved with another.

Adalric's hum came through the line. "Take a deep breath, and clear your mind," he ordered soothingly. "That was a long time ago." After a few seconds, he asked, "It *was*, wasn't it?"

Spieron grunted, then sucked in a harsh breath and did as his master recommended. "Yes," he responded after a moment. "Albert has been living alone in the mountains for the last five years. That's why I needed to get a new phone. To get coverage here, so I can stay with him and woo him."

"Of course." Adalric hummed softly for a few seconds before telling him, "Take all the time you need, but stay in touch. If problems arise, we are here to help."

While Spieron had expected that response, he still felt a wash of relief. "Thank you." Then he cleared his throat, knowing he had to share the possibility. "Nicholas is attempting to talk his father into returning to the ranch."

"Ahhh, so you may end up in Texas for a while," Adalric mused. "Is that what you're telling me?"

"Yes, Master Adalric."

"As long as I am master of the Esson coven, you will always have a place here, Spieron," Adalric told him calmly. Then his tone warmed. "In fact, with you there rubbing shoulders with a gargoyle elder . . . hmmm . . . that could be good for us."

Spieron barked a laugh, grinning widely. "I suppose that would definitely be a plus," he conceded.

Adalric chuckled, too. "Well, it certainly doesn't hurt. Now then, good luck, Spieron. Call if you need anything, and keep me apprised."

"I will, Master. Thank you."

"Congratulations again." Then Adalric disconnected the line.

Spieron rested the phone on his thigh and stared around the small clearing, grinning at nothing.

"Call go well then?"

Turning his attention to Elder Bodb, Spieron nodded. The elder rested against the side of the cabin, his wings wrapped around his shoulders. With them being in a secluded area, the gargoyle had taken to staying in his true form. Spieron bet living mostly as a human on the ranch would soon tire the huge male.

At least Albert had taken Bodb's true form in stride. That was probably due to Spieron scaring the shit out of him that first day.

Not my finest moment.

"Glad to hear it." Bodb pulled his phone from a satchel he had slung over his head and one shoulder. "Give me your new number." After Spieron obeyed, the gargoyle told him, "Nick says he's been working on getting his father to at least visit, but the man's become set in his ways after all this time." Bodb grimaced before adding, "I also think there are certain people he doesn't want to run into there, if you know what I mean."

Spieron nodded as he rubbed his fingers over his forehead. He understood that. If he'd had an affair with someone, producing a son he couldn't acknowledge, Spieron wouldn't want to see the woman, either.

"Is Albert over her?" Spieron blurted out the question without much thought. He hadn't considered that before. "What if he doesn't want to go back because he still wants her?"

Bodb lifted one eyebrow ridge, then rolled one shoulder in a half-shrug. "I can't answer that," he admitted. "That'd be something you'd need to ask directly."

Nodding again, Spieron commented, "Just thinking out loud, I guess."

It was Bodb's turn to nod. "We leave tomorrow morning. Are you sure you don't mind us taking your truck?"

In fact, Spieron *did* mind, but he wasn't going to tell Bodb that. "I'll pick it up eventually," he stated instead. "You can be certain of that."

Bodb hummed. "Nice evasion."

Spieron snickered. "Thanks."

The following morning was subdued.

Nicholas asked one last time for Albert to join them. "Please, Dad. You don't have to live out here like this." He swung his hand, indicating the wood pile, which was always in need of replenishment. Then Nicholas pointed at the workshop where Albert repaired traps and cared for his catches. "Come home."

Albert pulled Nicholas into his arms, hugging him. "I know you don't understand, son, but this *is* my home." Then he patted Nicholas's back before releasing him. "But it's been a long time since I've had a vacation. Maybe I'll plan for one." His bearded lips curved into a warm smile. "Will that appease you?"

"For now," Nicholas replied, his brown eyes gleaming. He blinked swiftly as he told him, "I love you, Dad. Always have, even when I thought you were my uncle."

Albert smiled and nodded. "I love you, too, son. I've always been proud of you."

Nicholas smiled again, then headed toward the truck. As he moved, he called over his shoulder, "Take good care of my dad, Spieron."

Spieron smirked as he called back, "You know I have every intention of doing that, Nick." He filled his tone with lustful innuendo as he peered at Albert hungrily.

Beneath Albert's beard, Spieron noticed the rising blush to his beloved's cheeks.

So fucking sexy.

"It was nice meeting you." Elder Bodb held out his hand to Albert. After they shook, he commented, "We look forward to hearing when you plan to take that vacation."

After Albert had nodded, he softly ordered, "Take care of my son."

Bodb gave Albert a wicked grin, then headed toward the truck as he laughed.

Once again, Albert's cheeks darkened, the color just visible beneath his thick salt and pepper beard.

Spieron loved that look on Albert so damn much. Leaning against the small pile of wood near the front door, he watched as Bodb climbed into the cab behind the wheel and fired up his vehicle. As the vehicle headed toward the bend in the dirt and gravel road, Spieron couldn't resist reaching out and gripping Albert's hand.

To Spieron's pleasure, Albert didn't fight him as he tugged him closer, so he could wrap his arm around his waist. In silence, they watched as Nicholas stuck his arm out of the passenger window and waved good-bye. Albert returned the gesture. Before long, the truck disappeared from view.

Just that fast, Spieron felt Albert yank from his grip. He lifted his brows in surprise as his beloved turned and pinned him with a nearly feral expression. His dark eyes gleamed beneath his brows, and he growled low in his throat.

Lifting his hands in placation, Spieron tried to figure out the sudden change. He'd seen no interaction that hinted at such an attitude. While Spieron knew Albert couldn't truly hurt him as a vampire—not physically, anyway—he wondered what was going on in his human's head.

If we were bonded, I'd know . . . because we'd have a mind-link. Shit! Did I explain that to him?

Spieron couldn't remember, and the thought swiftly slipped from his mind. He suddenly pegged the expression on Albert's face when his human peeled his lips from his teeth and growled low in his throat. His man was hungry . . . and judging from the delicious smell of desire that wafted to Spieron's nostrils, he didn't need food.

"Albert?" Spieron licked his lips, his gut clenching at the way his beloved swept his gaze down his body, then back up again. His blood swiftly heated and flowed south, flooding his cock. "Something on your mind, beloved?"

"You've been touching me an awful lot over the last few days, Spieron," Albert stated gruffly. His hands clenched and relaxed at his sides, and his body appeared to almost vibrate. "I *know* what you've been doing."

Spieron lifted his brows in question. "And what have I been doing?"

"You're a fucking cock-tease is what you are," Albert stated on a snarl.

Shaking his head, Spieron lowered his voice to a purring rumble as he replied, "My beloved, I am *not* a cock-tease. I would have been happy to relieve the pressure any time you wished."

Albert took a slow, stalking step forward. Since he was a couple of inches taller than Spieron's own six-foot-one frame, he had to look up at him. Resting his hands on a log on either side of his hips, he barely resisted the urge to grab his human. Spieron waited, hoping and praying this was going in the direction he thought it was.

"You know we couldn't," Albert snapped, stalking closer. "Not with Nicholas here."

Humming, Spieron smirked. He arched his back a little, knowing the move stretched his torso and put his swollen groin on blatant display. "Oh, Albert. Surely you don't think Nick and Bodb were celibate this week." Upon seeing the way Albert's brows shot up and how his head tipped, Spieron realized Albert had thought just that. "Surely you didn't think they needed to go to the outhouse together . . . or pump water from the well . . . and their daily evening walks beneath the stars?" Spieron offered Bodb a feral smile of his own. "While I figured you couldn't smell the residual scent of spent cum on their skin like I could, I thought you'd have put it together. Those two fuck like bunnies." Lowering his voice huskily, he added, "And I was so damn jealous of them. Are we about to fix that?"

Albert stared at him in shock for one heartbeat, then a second. Finally, he shook his head, and for one heart-stopping second, Spieron thought Albert was calling off whatever he had intended to start.

Thank the gods, I was wrong.

To Spieron's relief, Albert took that last step to close the distance between them. He spread his legs a little, putting their groins at the same level. Then he rocked forward while placing his hands on the wood behind either side of Spieron's hips.

Spieron groaned low in his throat upon feeling the exquisite pressure to his hard shaft. His hips bucked on instinct, and he rutted against Albert. His beloved met his movements, causing pleasant tendrils to spiral through his groin, radiating outward.

"Well, I'm glad I didn't realize it," Albert stated, a growl in his voice. "He's my son, so—" He shrugged.

"Got it," Spieron muttered, wondering how the hell Albert could still be forming coherent thoughts. He thought about how he could change that.

Spieron lifted his hands, intending to reach for Albert. His beloved growled and jerked his head, shaking it. "Put them back, Spieron. Now."

Even as Spieron's eyebrows shot up, he obeyed. No way in hell had he realized his human had such a dominant streak. To Spieron's surprise, the realization caused the hairs on his nape to stand on end and goose bumps to form on his arms. His heart felt as if it skipped a beat.

Hot damn!

"So, Spieron," Albert growled out. "You said you'd do anything for me."

As Albert spoke, he began to increase his thrusts.

Spieron groaned at the bliss-inducing stimulation. His mouth went dry, and he struggled to catch his breath. He found his gaze straying to Albert's lips, and he desperately wanted a taste.

"Well?" Albert stilled his hips, and when Spieron continued his ruts, he moved his hands to his hips. His fingers dug in, hard, causing Spieron to still and snap his focus back to Albert's eyes. "Well, Spieron? Would you do anything for me?"

"Damn near about," Spieron finally managed to reply.

"Near about?" Albert narrowed his eyes. "What's off the table?"

Spieron knew he had to tell the truth. "Walking away from you. I can't do it."

Albert hummed as a wide smile curved his whisker-covered face. "Then it's a good thing that's not what I was going to ask." He began moving his hips again as he pressed closer, bringing their chests flush together. "I want," he began on a whisper as he wrapped his arms around Spieron's waist and rubbed his palms up his back. Once Albert had dipped his head so his lips were so close to Spieron's ear that his breath tickled the fine hairs beneath it, Albert finished, "Your ass, Spieron. Give it to me."

Even as Spieron's gut clenched and his chute muscles quivered — he hadn't bottomed in nearly a century — he replied, "It's yours."

CHAPTER SIX

A ripple of excitement coursed through Albert. Letting it
out on a growl, he took a step backward. He heard Spieron's moan of disappointment, but he didn't dwell on it.

Instead, Albert grabbed Spieron's right wrist with his left
hand. Then he bent at the waist. Grabbing the vampire's hip
with his free hand, he pulled the man forward. When he
straightened, Albert easily hefted him onto his shoulder.

Albert felt just a twinge from his muscles, reminding him
he wasn't as young as he used to be. Ignoring it, he used his
booted foot to shove open his cabin's cracked-open door the
rest of the way. He strode through his home, doing his best
to ignore the way his throbbing shaft rubbed against the fly
of his jeans with each step he took.

While on his walks with Nicholas, Albert had asked plenty of questions about not only gargoyles and vampires, but
about the whole mating thing that happened between them.
His son had assured him that, regardless of what Albert
needed, his vampire would do his damnedest to provide it.
Albert hadn't been so sure, but he'd been willing to try.

Having his dick hard as a steel pipe any time he was
around the vampire had been disconcerting at first. He
wasn't a young man, and he couldn't remember the last time
he'd gotten so hard so fast. Hell, even when he *was* a young
man, he hadn't ever felt so randy.

If Albert was honest with himself, he liked it . . . a lot!

Albert maneuvered them into the cabin's single
bedroom—a room his guests had refused to enter, calling it

his sanctuary. In truth, he'd appreciated that. Having a place to hide away had helped him keep his sanity.

Living alone for five years, then suddenly having unexpected guests—even family—well, he just hadn't been prepared for it.

Bending at his waist, Albert placed Spieron on his bed. He had to admit that he felt a bit surprised that the man hadn't said anything about his manhandling. For his bed-partners in the past, Albert's desire to control their encounters had caused tension.

Spieron didn't seem to have a problem with it, at all. In fact, the vampire sprawled where Albert had put him. He even rested his hands behind his head and grinned broadly up at him, lust radiating from his expression.

Fucking hell, that's sexy.

"Stay still," Albert ordered.

"Anything you want, my beloved."

The throaty rumble of Spieron's reply went straight to Albert's dick, and his desire rushed through him so hard his cock twitched and his balls ached. Groaning, he reached down and pressed the heel of his palm to the base of his erection. He pressed, hard, stemming his need to come.

"Damn, Albert," Spieron stated, his grin showing off his sharp fangs. "The things I could do with what you're packing. I could make you blow and still keep you hard."

Albert lifted a brow even as he reached for Spieron's boot. "I highly doubt that," he countered as he removed the other man's boots and socks. "I'm not a young man, Spieron." Recalling who he was talking to, someone over a hundred and thirty years old, Albert scoffed before adding, "In human terms, I'm over the hill."

"And yet, I could *still* do as I said," Spieron countered. "Perhaps after you fuck me through the mattress, I'll prove it to you." His eyes narrowed even as he lifted his hips, allowing Albert to open his fly and pull his jeans down and off. "While I have no desire to hear about your past conquests, I love a challenge. What's your record?"

Albert's thoughts stalled in his mind. Spieron had gone commando, and the vampire's long, slender prick jutted up from his groin. His soon-to-be lover even spread his legs, putting his heavy balls as well as his tight hole on clear display.

Moaning, Albert once again fought his need for release. He yanked open his fly, then thrust his hand down his pants. Grabbing his balls, he squeezed and twisted.

Albert panted harshly as a shudder worked through him. The pain only eased his need a little, and he struggled to catch his breath. He gritted his teeth as he peeled open eyelids he hadn't realized he'd closed.

Fucking hell!

Spieron had stripped his shirt on his own and lay sprawled naked in the middle of his bed. His legs were splayed, and one of his hands was up beneath his head. With his free hand, he gripped his dick in what appeared to be a loose hold, and he was jacking it slowly.

Pre-cum beaded at the tip.

Albert moaned as his dick twitched, a matching pearl of pre-cum oozing from him.

"What'd you do to me?" Albert blurted out his question, but he figured it was a valid comment. He'd never felt like this before.

"I warned you," Spieron answered huskily. "The longer we're together and don't complete the bond, the more our arousal and need for each other will dominate our bodies to the point of distraction." His expression sobered as he told him, "I told you Fate likes to get her way."

"Fate . . . just fuck." Albert scowled at him even as he unbuttoned the top couple of buttons on his flannel shirt. "We don't know two shits about each other," he pointed out before whipping the fabric over his head.

"That will change," Spieron countered, seeming to be completely unconcerned.

Hell, he grew up with this shit. It probably doesn't concern him at all.

While toeing off his boots, Albert muttered, "You said you could get me off and still leave me hard enough to fuck you." He couldn't believe he was contemplating it, but his dick seemed to be doing the thinking.

"Oh, yes, beloved." Spieron sounded so damn certain, his expression containing a mixture of hunger and smugness. "We will not leave this bed until you've fucked me through the mattress as often as you want, and we are a tired, sweaty mess."

"Don't know if I'd want to leave the bed if that were the case," Albert grumbled, shoving off his jeans.

Spieron laughed, his pleasure lighting his features.

The mirthful movement also opened Spieron's mouth, and Albert's gut clenched with his desires. Giving in to his need, he crawled onto the bed. He held the vampire's gaze as he prowled to the head of the bed.

Grabbing a pillow with one hand, Albert slid his other under Spieron's head. He gently massaged the man's scalp, enjoying the soft strands of his thick auburn hair as he lifted. Sliding the pillow under Spieron's head, Albert put it at the angle he wanted.

Albert released Spieron, then slung his leg over the other man's torso. Grabbing the headboard, he arched his back. The move caused his jutting erection to dangle just before Spieron's mouth.

"Suck me." Albert snarled the order even as his cock twitched before the other man's lips. It took every bit of his self-control to keep from bumping his crown against Spieron's lips and insisting.

To Albert's relief, Spieron didn't even hesitate. He opened wide, lifted his head, and wrapped his lips around Albert's bulbous head. Feeling the strong sucking pulls and seeing Spieron's mouth on him, Albert felt his balls roll.

Clenching his teeth, Albert tried to hang on.

When Albert felt Spieron's hands grip his upper thighs, his thumbs bumping and nudging at his balls, his control snapped. He clenched his hands on the headboard as a deep growl tore from his throat. Snapping his hips, Albert buried his cock deep into Spieron's throat again and again.

Spieron never once shied away. In fact, he hummed and sucked. He used his tongue to massage Albert's throbbing vein. He even managed to swallow around his head each time Albert thrust forward and lodged his crown into Spieron's throat.

Grunting harshly, Albert felt his balls pull tight. His bliss crested, and his orgasm swamped his senses. Shuddering hard, his cock pulsing, he poured his release down his lover's throat.

Albert would have felt bad that he hadn't offered any warning, but considering the way Spieron moaned and continued sucking, he guessed the man didn't mind so much. Even as he opened his mouth to comment—it was only polite to apologize, after all, even if it was after the fact—Spieron hummed as he lapped along Albert's still-throbbing vein. Instead of words, a groan was ripped from Albert's throat.

Then the sharp spike of teeth sinking into the vein running the length of his dick shot a stab of pain through Albert. He sucked in a harsh breath, getting ready to blast the vampire for his asshole-ish-ness. Except, in the next instant, the most exquisite pulse of bliss rocked through his groin, and his balls pulled tight as a second orgasm crashed through him, blindsiding him.

Roaring, Albert felt his hips buck spastically as his head swam. He rested his forehead on the wall, still gripping the headboard, and struggled to get enough air into his lungs. The black spots dancing behind his eyes made thinking tough, and he didn't fight the trembles as he floated on endorphins from the best damn double-orgasm he'd ever experienced.

Albert slowly came back to himself . . . mostly because his overly sensitive prick throbbed with each lap of Spieron's tongue against his frenulum. Forcing his eyelids open, Albert peered down at the vampire. The male somehow managed to smirk around Albert's piece of meat where it still rested in his mouth.

How could a man look so damn smug while sucking cock?

While Albert didn't know, Spieron still managed to pull it off. *And damn it all, my dick is still hard!* Albert could hardly believe that, either.

Even as Albert acknowledged that fact, said prick twitched in Spieron's mouth. His original desire surged through him like a tsunami. Albert wanted to fuck his lover through the mattress so damn bad he could almost taste it.

Albert growled low in his throat as he pushed away from the headboard. The move pulled his dick out of Spieron's mouth, and his erection immediately bobbed up, slapping wetly against his stomach. The tingles created shot through his groin, sending a zing to his testicles.

"Holy fucking shit," Albert muttered as he slung his leg over and moved off of Spieron's torso.

Spieron grinned up at him, his expression almost cheeky. "How you feelin' now, Albert?" Reaching out, he skimmed his forefingers up the underside of Albert's still-bobbing shaft. "Better?"

"You know I am," Albert snarled, knocking Spieron's hand away. "What the fuck were you thinking? Biting my dick?"

Laughing huskily, Spieron waggled his brows. "Vampire." Then he winked. "And my bite will always get you off . . . no matter where I sink my fangs." As he spoke, he touched the underside of Albert's ball sack.

Albert sucked in a harsh gasp as he eased away from Spieron. "No fucking way."

Spieron laughed again even as he nodded his head.

Albert didn't know if the way his heart tripped in his chest was caused by fear or anticipation. Shaking his head, he reached for the nightstand drawer. Either way, it wasn't happening right then.

Grabbing the tube of lubricant that he occasionally used to jack off — *god, when was the last time I bothered* — Albert closed the drawer. Once he'd positioned himself between his lover's legs and popped the cap, he froze.

Wait a minute.

"Albert?" Spieron ran his palm down his chest, pausing to tease along his ribcage. "What is it, my beloved?"

Albert snapped his attention back to Spieron. He had no idea how long he'd been staring at the wall, but during that time, his lover had risen onto one elbow. Spieron even sported a concerned expression.

"If you've changed your mind —" Spieron began, but Albert cut him off.

"I haven't, but —" Albert cleared his throat in discomfort. He felt his cheeks heat, which was something that seemed to happen way too often around the vampire. "You wouldn't happen to have a condom, would you?"

It had obviously been far too long since he'd nearly forgotten that standard piece of equipment.

Spieron smiled even as he shook his head. "No need for that, Albert," he told him as he continued to pet along his ribcage and up his chest. "I'm a vampire. A paranormal. Even if you have something, and if you do, we'll discuss it later, I cannot get or give human diseases." As he slid his hand down and began to glide his palm over the soft skin of Albert's slightly softened belly, Spieron continued, "There will never be a need for condoms between us." He offered Albert a feral smile. "I can't wait to feel your hard, heavy shaft moving within me." Reaching down, Spieron gripped said erection and began jacking him. "Glorious."

Albert groaned and jerked backward, out of Spieron's hold. He couldn't believe it, but his lover's touch had already drawn a pearl of pre-cum from him. Beads of sweat broke out on his torso as he struggled to control himself.

So fucking crazy!

Taking Spieron at his word, Albert poured a dollop of slick onto his fingers. He closed the tube and tossed it aside as he spread the lubricant over his digits, warming the cool liquid. Then he peered down at Spieron's tiny opening and gulped hard.

Still, Albert's dominant personality wouldn't allow him to stop. He recalled every instance of stretching he'd ever seen in the gay porn he'd watched as he lowered his fingertips to Spieron's opening. Teasing over the flesh, he massaged and pushed, dipping just the tip of one finger, then another, into his lover's body.

After a moment of play, Spieron growled, drawing Albert's attention. He sucked in a breath upon seeing the vampire's eyes bleed to red. To his surprise, instead of fear, a wave of pride crashed through Albert.

I did that. I caused this vampire to lose himself to his need.

"Something wrong?" Albert couldn't help but tease.

"Fucking put it in me already," Spieron demanded.

Albert grinned. "Say please."

Spieron hissed as he rocked his hips, pushing his ass into Albert's teasing touches. When after a few seconds Albert only gave him glancing stretches, Spieron finally snarled, "Please, goddammit!"

Chuckling roughly, Albert gave Spieron what he wanted and sank his middle finger as deeply into his channel as he could. While hearing Spieron groan with pleasure, Albert let out a moan of his own. His erection twitched, and his gut clenched.

Never had Albert felt such tight heat.

I want, need *to get in here.*

With that one thought dominating his mind, Albert began stretching his new lover in earnest.

CHAPTER SEVEN

Spieron reveled in the sensations racking his body. The stretch caused by Albert's fingers in his chute created the slightest burn, sending zings through his groin. His cock throbbed with each nudge to his prostate.

Best of all, however, was the hungry, lustful, needy expression etched on his beloved's features.

My human needs, and I will provide.

Rubbing his palms down Albert's thickly muscled arms, Spieron admired his powerful limbs. "I'm ready," he rasped, his voice rough from having his lover's dick repeatedly shoved into his throat. Knowing he'd driven his human beyond control had made it more than worth it. "Fuck me, Albert. Give me your cock."

Albert paused in his ministrations, and a tremble worked through him. He lifted his gaze from where he'd been staring at his fingers in Spieron's chute. Meeting his gaze, Albert's expression took on a hint of confliction.

"Your opening is so small," Albert mumbled, glancing down once more before meeting Spieron's gaze. "How will I fit?"

It suddenly hit Spieron—Albert's dominance in the bedroom had hidden his inexperience.

Up until now, anyway.

Seeing that Albert needed reassurance, Spieron squeezed his chute muscles around his lover's three digits as he held his beloved's gaze. He noticed the way Albert's nostrils flared and his lips twisted. His man's big body even shuddered.

"My body was made to fit yours," Spieron told him. *Well, technically, it's probably the other way around, since I'm older, but whatever.* Pushing the stray thought aside, Spieron gave Albert a hungry smile of his own. "Trust me, my beloved." Spieron slid his hands to Albert's chest, exploring through the springy curls of his chest hair, so different from his own smooth chest. "Give us what we both need."

A low, needy groan rumbled from Albert's chest, and Spieron felt the vibration through his fingers. As he felt Albert ease his fingers from his body, he knew his human was giving in to his lust. As Spieron watched, Albert lifted away from him and rested on his calves, only to grab the tube of slick from where he'd dropped it on the mattress.

Spieron's breath caught in his throat as he admired the man Fate had given to him.

Albert's thighs bulged, and his shoulders were so very broad. His pectorals were clearly defined even under the salt and pepper coating of his chest hair. His treasure trail traveled over a smooth belly and led to a thick thatch of dark curls.

Licking his lips as he watched Albert coat his long, fat prick with lubricant, Spieron remembered how his human's dick had felt in his mouth and tasted on his tongue. It had been the epitome of tastefulness. His flesh's deep masculine flavor had caused his taste buds to sing, and the taste of his cream mixed with blood had nearly caused him to blow his own load.

Only a swift squeeze to the base of his prick had stopped his orgasm. Although in hindsight, he probably should have just let go.

Next time.

"Fuck, the way you look at me," Albert snarled as he released his cock. "Need. Now."

"Yessss," Spieron hissed, reaching for Albert as he levered

over him. "Fucking now."

Albert rested his weight on his left elbow as he reached between them with his right. Spieron felt the nudge of his lover's broad head against his opening and locked his gaze on his human's eyes which appeared to glow with need. When he felt the pressure of Albert pushing against him, Spieron pushed out.

Spieron felt his body give way, and his muscles stretched . . . and stretched. He reminded himself to stay relaxed, but it was damn tough. As Albert sank deeper and deeper inside him, he almost felt as if he were being split wide open.

Only the look of absolute rapture on Albert's face gave Spieron the control to keep his discomfort from his face.

Finally, Albert bottomed out, but he didn't stop. He eased partway out, then pushed back in. After several more strokes, he buried himself balls deep and stopped.

Spieron trembled under Albert, clinging to the man. His fingers slid over his lover's sweat-slicked skin, and he felt his human press his forehead against his shoulder. A hard shudder worked through the body above him.

"S-Spieron," Albert ground out on a groan. "Holy shit!"

Rubbing his hands up and down Albert's damp spine, Spieron kept himself breathing. To his relief, the pain ebbed swiftly. He turned his head and nipped at Albert's ear.

"You okay?" Spieron whispered when Albert still didn't move.

Albert nodded, his face rubbing against Spieron's skin, although he stayed quiet.

Concern sliding through him, Spieron massaged the backs of Albert's shoulders as he pressed light kisses to the side of Albert's bearded face. He felt his beloved's prick twitch within him, but his lover remained still. His body continued to shudder, however.

"Talk to me, my beloved," Spieron crooned. His own dick throbbed between them. Even the discomfort caused by Albert entering and rutting hadn't diminished his hardness. "What's wrong?"

A low groan erupted from Albert. "Nothing wrong," he muttered roughly. "I-If I move"—he paused as he shivered again—"gonna come and don't want to."

Spieron grinned as a low chuckle erupted from him. "That's a fantastic problem to have," he purred into Albert's ear. "Move, beloved. Please, move. I want to feel your cum filling my chute, warming me from the inside."

When Albert continued to remain still, Spieron decided to up his game. He clenched and released his chute muscles, beginning a rhythmic massage to his beloved's embedded erection. It only took half a dozen pulses before Spieron got exactly what he wanted.

A tortured moan burst from Albert, and he began to move. He pulled out, then slammed back into Spieron. He began a punishing pace, rutting into him with little finesse—just raw power driven by need.

Spieron reveled in the feeling his lover's wanton abandon. Lifting his legs, he wrapped them around his beloved. He wrapped his arms around Albert and used his hold to rock into each of his thrusts.

The change in angle caused Albert's cock head to slide over his prostate with each rut. Fiery tendrils erupted through his groin, and it was Spieron's turn to groan lustily. The smell of sweat and arousal filled his senses, and his body swam with rising bliss.

Between the sensations created by Albert reaming his ass and the feel of his dick rubbing against his beloved's hairy torso, Spieron became lost. The base of his spine tingled. His balls tightened.

"Albert!" Spieron roared as his orgasm burst upon him.

Wave upon wave of ecstasy coursed through his body. "Yessss!"

Spieron bucked in Albert's hold, and his lover slid a thick arm under him as he slammed into him one last time, holding him close. Feeling Albert's dick pulse inside his channel, he hummed appreciatively, loving that his beloved marked him so intimately. He scented the sweet, iron-rich blood pounding up Albert's neck, and his mouth watered.

Acting on instincts that his blissed-out brain couldn't control, Spieron opened his mouth and sank his fangs into his beloved's flesh. His human's sweet nectar poured across his tongue. He groaned as he enjoyed Albert's succulent flavor, wiping his tongue around his teeth as he sucked for more.

Albert cried out, the sound one of ecstasy. His cock pulsed once more inside Spieron's chute, again coating his insides with his seed.

Coming back to himself, Spieron carefully eased his teeth from Albert's skin. He licked over the bite marks, sealing the holes his fangs had made and wiping away the last traces of his beloved's blood. After swallowing those few drops, Spieron hummed appreciatively as he nuzzled his smooth cheek against Albert's fuzzy one.

"Amazing," Albert slurred. His big body lay heavy on Spieron, totally relaxed. "H-How the hell d-did you do that to m-me?"

Spieron massaged his lover's back with his palms, mapping him with his fingertips. "Mmm, *you* are amazing," he replied, uncertain what his lover had meant. "Do what?"

The feel of Albert's muscles under flesh moving beneath his palms added to Spieron's pleasure. The simple action of being able to touch his beloved created a contentment that Spieron hadn't expected to feel. No one had ever mentioned it to him, anyway, but he sure loved it.

"Y-You asked what my r-record was." Albert began to

shift his body, but Spieron held him tight.

"Stay," Spieron urged, absently recalling their stalled conversation from earlier.

Albert lifted his head and peered down at him. "Surely I'm way too heavy for this to be comfortable," he said with furrowed brows.

Spieron smiled lethargically. "Vampire, remember? I'm far stronger than I look."

His expression eased, and he returned Spieron's smile. "Huh." Then he completely relaxed against him, giving his weight back over to him. "Gotta admit. This is nice." He wriggled his hips a little as he turned his head and met Spieron's gaze. He even waggled his eyebrows. "Never been able to just leave my dick in someone like this. It's fucking fantastic."

Laughing softly, Spieron asked, "So what was your record for one evening?" He had a funny idea that he'd already blown it away.

"Two," Albert admitted. "And they sure weren't back to back. It was with—"

"Stop there," Spieron countered, squeezing his lover's hip. "No names. I don't want to have to fight my instincts to rip their eyes out if I ever meet them."

Albert's lips parted in surprise, but he did as he was told. "O-Okay."

Spieron realized he needed to explain. "Paranormals, in general, are damn jealous when it comes to their significant others." Rubbing up and down Albert's spine, he added, "And no way are we done for the day, no matter what your prick is telling you right now."

Snorting, Albert again began to move, and that time, Spieron let him. His beloved flopped to his left. He huffed a sigh, then reached out and slid his left arm under Spieron. Bending his elbow, Albert rolled him, causing him to sprawl over him.

While Spieron found the position odd, he went with it. Being a pretty powerful vampire in his own right—he had earned an enforcer position within his coven, after all—it was a position he wasn't familiar with. Still, having him pressed up close to Albert and cuddling into his side seemed to make his beloved especially happy.

That gave Spieron a sense of satisfaction.

For a long moment, they lay quietly together. Spieron listened to the steady thump of Albert's heart beneath his ear. His pulse slowed, and he felt the lethargy that came after a great orgasm begin to creep up on him.

Spieron had closed his eyes and begun to doze when Albert spoke.

"You bit me . . . a couple of times."

Grunting acknowledgement, Spieron peeled his eyelids open and met Albert's gaze. He saw the questions there, so he waited for his beloved to voice them. His man took a few seconds to work them out.

"Does that mean we're bonded?"

Spieron should have realized that would be something a human would consider. He couldn't lie to him, either. His beloved needed all the facts.

Before Spieron could decide on how to explain, Albert added, "I asked Nick about how a vampire bonds, but since he's attached to a gargoyle, he wasn't certain."

"Gargoyle bonding is more involved, I hear," Spieron murmured, rubbing his hand over his lover's chest. His fingertips ran across the slight crustiness caused by his drying cum. Ignoring it in favor of continuing the moment with his beloved, Spieron stated, "A vampire must claim his beloved through sex, me spilling in you." As he spoke, he teased his fingertips along the crease of Albert's groin, so his meaning couldn't be misinterpreted. "And biting you during sex, so yes . . . I did start our bond." Meeting Albert's dark eyes, Spieron added, "But our connection began the second we laid eyes on each other."

Albert sighed deeply and fell silent.

Spieron allowed it for several minutes, until the itching on his groin and stomach grew uncomfortable. The feel of his lover's seed oozing from his ass was also an unfamiliar sensation. Considering his human's pushiness in the bedroom, Spieron figured he would have to get used to that, though.

Not a hardship, though. My man's dick is a thing of beauty.

"I'm gonna get us a cloth to clean us up," Spieron murmured, then lifted onto his elbow and tipped forward. He dipped his head and pressed a kiss to Albert's lips.

Spieron had intended for it to be a chaste brush of lips, but the second his mouth touched his lover's, Albert grunted and moved his right hand to Spieron's nape. Albert's hand tightened on both his nape and around his waist. His beloved began mapping his mouth, sliding his tongue deep and even teasing along his fangs.

When Albert scraped his tongue along his pointed canine, Spieron fed his lover a groan.

Albert snapped his head back and grinned at him. "Like that, do you?"

"Hell yeah," Spieron immediately admitted. "My fangs are sensitive."

"Excellent," Albert muttered, his dark eyes gleaming as his expression once again grew hungry. "Like knowing I make you just as crazy as you make me."

The smell of Albert's renewed arousal reached Spieron's senses, and his body answered. His blood heated within him and flowed south. In seconds, his erection throbbed, and he rubbed it against Albert's hip.

"Skip the clean-up," Albert stated, then pushed Spieron away.

Before Spieron could voice his surprise, Albert sat up and

grabbed his hips. With surprising strength, his lover flipped him. Once Spieron lay on his stomach, Albert covered him, pushing his knees between Spieron's own, forcing his legs apart.

Spieron grinned as he acquiesced. He felt his beloved's cock head prod at his entrance once more. Canting his hips, he made certain his human knew his taking was welcome.

Except, Albert paused.

Peering over his shoulder, Spieron saw the way Albert peered down at his ass. His look was one of . . . smug pride. Then Spieron felt Albert's finger slide around his rim, the way made easy by the cum still dribbling from him and the remains of the slick.

Albert teased his finger into Spieron's body, pressing against his prostate.

Spieron groaned and pushed back as Albert pulled his finger away.

"That's so fucking sexy," Albert murmured. "My cum is dripping from you, and I'm gonna fill you with more."

"Yesss," Spieron hissed. "Do it."

"Your body is mine, isn't it?" Albert asked even as he positioned his dick and sank into Spieron, letting out a husky groan as he did so.

"All yours."

Albert lay over Spieron's body — his cock buried deep. He rubbed his face against the back of Spieron's neck, teasing the sensitive skin there with his beard. A shiver worked down Spieron's spine, causing his chute muscles to ripple.

"Yeah, you like that," Albert rumbled, letting out a throaty chuckle.

"Love your dick in me and your hands on me any way I can get them," Spieron stated.

"Good," Albert stated as he began to rut. "Because I'm getting used to the feel of your ass around my dick, and I ain't comin' out any time soon."

Spieron chuckled at that visual, but the noise instantly morphed into a moan as Albert began pegging his prostate with each move his glorious erection made.

CHAPTER EIGHT

A lbert rubbed the back of his neck, massaging down it, then working over his shoulder. The hairs on his nape stood on end when his fingertips skimmed over the claiming scar on his neck. His stomach clenched on instinct, and his blood began to heat and flow south.

Yanking his hand away from his neck, Albert shook his head.

Three weeks.

Three weeks of sex with Spieron and still his body felt on edge . . . primed . . . as if he was waiting for something.

As Albert saddled his horse, he had to acknowledge what it was, too—at least mentally. His lover had explained it . . . more than once. The longer they stayed together without completing their bond, the more his body's needs would come to distract him.

"Sure you don't want me to come?" Spieron asked from directly behind him.

Albert didn't jump. He'd known the vampire was there. Over the last few weeks, he'd somehow managed to develop a sixth sense about where his lover was.

Turning, Albert smiled. "I won't be gone long. Two hours tops." Seeing Spieron open his mouth, probably to question him some more, Albert lifted his hand to stop him. He chuckled as he watched Spieron snap his mouth shut. "Relax. I just need to check my hog trap." Grinning, he winked. "If we're lucky, we'll have fresh liver and onions for supper."

Spieron nodded even as he reached out and slid his fingers through Albert's hair. When his lover cradled his head and urged him down, Albert went with it. He kissed his vampire slowly, enjoying the tongue-play . . . especially when he scraped over one fang, sending a shiver down his spine.

Jerking away, Albert caressed Spieron's jaw. "Knock that off, handsome," he rumbled. "If I don't leave now, I won't be back before dark." A fresh wave of lust surged through him when he thought about why he was getting a late start. "We fuck like bunnies, and it's still not enough."

Sighing, Spieron nodded as he stepped backward. "And you know why that is."

Albert swallowed hard as he worked his jaw. "I know why that is." Then he turned and led his horses from the small paddock by the reins of the first one. The second animal he used primarily for packing, and it followed docilely behind the first, not even putting tension on its lead line. After swinging into the saddle, Albert bent and pressed one more hard, fast kiss to Spieron's lips. "Be back before ya know it."

Then Albert nudged his horse with his heels and started him trotting out of the yard. He gave in and looked back, seeing Spieron leaning against the fence rail. The look of longing on his lover's face sent a pang of remorse surging through him.

"Damn it," Albert grumbled to himself as he focused on the trail ahead. "Why the hell am I fighting this so hard?"

Why am I?

After being used by Katrina, Albert had sworn off all relationships beyond his son, nephews, and the ranch foreman. It had worked for decades, too. For a long time, Albert hadn't thought he'd had a heart anymore.

With the gap that had grown between himself and Vernon, then the strain on his relationship with Nicholas after Mitch had left Texas to lead his own life, walking away from the ranch hadn't been that difficult. Living alone had suited him.

Then Nicholas had shown up at his cabin door, and his life had been turned upside down

But it's a good change, isn't it? Spieron can't turn his back on you, and the issue with Katrina was your own damn fault.

But it gave me Nicholas.

And now you have a chance to have a real relationship with Nicholas. Why are you fighting this?

Albert scoffed as he realized he was having a mental debate with himself. "God, I really am such an ass."

As soon as Albert admitted that, *why* he was being an ass hit him square in the jaw — mentally speaking, anyway.

Well, fuck a duck!

The horse beneath him shied violently, and Albert started. Just as fast, his mount reared and pivoted. The rope attached to his pack horse twisted around his leg, and when his horse lunged forward, it tightened.

A low tree limb to the right side of the trail slammed into Albert's chest, brushing him from his horse's back. The rope around his leg kept him attached to the animal as it began galloping back toward the cabin. His head bounced on the ground once, making him see stars, before he gathered his wits enough to yank his knife from his belt.

Albert crunched up and slashed the blade through the rope, sending him tumbling to the ground. The pack horse, which was still following obediently, landed a hoof to his left upper thigh first, then the calf of his other leg. Pain speared through both limbs, and he roared.

Black spots floated before his visage as he rolled to a stop. The sound of pounding hooves disappeared in the distance. He forced himself to blink, to focus, knowing that passing out in the woods could be a death sentence.

Turning his head, Albert peered around warily. He spotted a pair of elk one hundred yards up the trail. The doe blinked at him slowly, then turned and disappeared into the trees, followed by her calf.

Albert groaned as he rolled onto his back. *That explains what spooked my horse.* Elk weren't native to Texas, but herds had been brought in and established, and they were beginning to spread.

Staring at the canopy above him, Albert took several slow, deep breaths. Then he planted his palms and forced himself to a sitting position. His head instantly swam, and he once again blinked swiftly and focused on breathing.

When Albert felt in control again, he opened eyelids he hadn't realized he'd closed. Spotting the blood soaking his right calf, he wished he hadn't looked. His stomach churned, and his head swam.

Living in the mountains, having to butcher his kills, the sight of blood had never bothered him. Seeing it oozing out of his own torn calf, however, was something different altogether.

Albert swallowed hard, then opened his eyes again. He forced himself to inspect his injuries. While the pants of his left thigh were torn, and there was blood seeping into the fabric, a quick inspection showed that it was just scraped — most likely from his pack horse's hoof sliding off his thick muscle. His right leg wasn't so lucky. Albert knew that one was broken. Having broken his wrist coming off a horse as a teenager, he knew what a broken bone felt like.

Also, the slight bulge under his skin was a dead give-away.

Even though Albert knew he needed to set the bone, as soon as he began feeling around the area, he realized he was in a world of trouble. With just the slightest push, his head began to swim again. Albert tried to control himself but failed.

Within seconds, Albert's eyes rolled to the back of his head, and he slumped to the ground.

The soft sound of beeping penetrated the fog blanketing his mind. He struggled to place it. At first, he thought it was his alarm, but then he remembered he hadn't used an alarm in decades.

Albert had always risen with the sun.

Attempting to open his eyelids proved difficult. They felt gummy and stiff. He tried again but to no success.

"Hey, handsome. Just relax."

Spieron's melodious tenor gave Albert something to focus on. He turned his head toward his lover. Feeling the squeeze to the fingers of his right hand, Albert realized Spieron had been holding his hand, so he squeezed back.

"I'm gonna get a cloth to wipe your eyes," Spieron murmured into his ear. "Just relax."

Since Albert couldn't seem to do much more than wiggle his fingers, he did as he was told. He listened, hearing the other man's soft footsteps. It wasn't the sound of the boots on the cabin's hardwood floor, though.

That was when Albert realized he smelled something odd, and it took him a second to place it.

Antiseptic?

Albert's memories came rushing back—his horse spooking, falling, getting dragged, and finally cutting himself free only to pass out from pain.

When the sound of running water turned off, Albert whispered, "I'm in the hospital. Aren't I?"

"Not currently," Spieron countered. "Do you remember what happened?"

"Yeah. Got distracted," Albert murmured. "Elk spooked my mount. Got tangled in my pack's lead line." Feeling Spieron's hand on his shoulder, he added, "I wanna blame you, because I was thinkin' about you. Our incomplete bond."

Spieron gently skimmed his fingers up until he teased at Albert's bearded cheek. "Hold still," he muttered right before the damp cloth touched Albert's face. As Spieron wiped at his eyes, he softly replied, "I'm sorry, my beloved."

Realizing how his words could have been taken, Albert forced open his freshly wiped eyes. He spotted Spieron's pained expression and wanted to kick his own ass. His words had hurt his lover.

Albert knew how to fix that, though.

Lifting his hand, Albert grabbed Spieron's wrist. "I'm sorry. I didn't mean it like that. It wasn't your fault." He smiled up at his lover, knowing he had to say the rest. "You found my heart again, and that realization distracted me. It was my fault. I would normally have had no trouble reining in my startled mount." Albert's brows drew together, and he found himself getting distracted. "Are my horses okay? How did I get here?" Glancing around, he was more than a little surprised to see that he wasn't in the sterile environs of a hospital room. He didn't recognize the room, however. "Where am I?"

"The ranch," Spieron told him, his features easing into a smile.

Albert glanced around again. "Was an expansion done?"

Spieron shrugged. "I don't know. This is a downstairs room in the main house." The vampire glanced around as if trying to figure out a better answer for him.

Lifting his hand, Albert grabbed Spieron's wrist. "I love you." Seeing the shock on his lover's face, he twisted his lips into a wry smile. "I think that's why I was fighting our connection so hard."

As Albert waited for an answer, he brought their twined hands to his lips and kissed Spieron's knuckles.

Spieron's nostrils flared, and his eyes bled red. Then he

blinked, and his smile held obvious disbelief. Settling on the side of the bed, he threaded the fingers of his free hand through Albert's hair.

"I love you, too, my beloved," Spieron responded sincerely. "But are you certain this isn't just your meds talking?"

"I'm on meds?" Albert blurted out the question before he could think better of it. Then he remembered the floaty feeling he'd had to fight through in order to reveal that he'd woken. "Of course, I am. I broke my leg."

Seeing Spieron's grimace, Albert heaved a sigh. Then he lifted his left hand, but he put it back down just as quickly. There was an IV in that arm.

"Shit, I hate needles," Albert mumbled, peering pointedly to the right and trying to forget what he'd just seen.

Spieron immediately let go of his hand, then reached over and pulled the blanket over his left arm. "Safe," he murmured.

Albert blinked, then focused on Spieron. "Did you just say you love me?"

Smirking, Spieron nodded. "Have for weeks, but it happens fast for paranormals. I wasn't certain if you would, or how long it would take. I—"

Lifting his hand, Albert grabbed Spieron again even as a wave of fatigue passed over him. "Damn, I'm tired." When he felt his vampire try to pull away, he growled. "Get in bed with me, then tell me how the hell I ended up here."

Spieron's soft chuckle reached Albert, making him smile. Feeling the bed to his right dip, he sighed. To Albert's relief, his lover crawled in beside him, and while he rested his hand on Albert's chest, he kept his lower half well away from him.

Albert was going to pull him closer, but then a throb in his right leg registered, telling him why his vampire was being so careful.

"When your horses came barreling into the yard without you, I damn near had a heart attack. Which shouldn't be possible for my kind, by the way." While Spieron's voice held a hint of mirth, there was strain there, too. "I raced down that trail as fast as I could, but still you'd already passed out by the time I got there."

"I'm sorry," Albert whispered absently, but the words seemed so inadequate.

Spieron growled softly. "It was an accident. They happen." His vampire didn't sound pleased by the admission, however. "While I can admit it, it doesn't make it any easier to accept. And if our bond had been complete, you could have called out to me via our telepathic bond. I would have been there sooner. I—"

"Stop, Spieron," Albert whispered. "It's my fault we aren't bonded. Not yours. I'm the one who kept putting you off." Heaving a deep sigh, he admitted, "I allowed my past issues with relationships to hold me back from something you offered so freely."

Spieron had explained the mind thingy to him, and it had been just another bit of weirdness that Albert had used to keep the vampire at arm's length.

"What's the rest of the story?" Albert asked, pressing for answers. They could talk about their relationship soon enough.

After I assimilate the wondrous fact that Spieron loves me.

"I called for an airlift, then I contacted Elder Bodb," Spieron told him as he rubbed his palm over Albert's bare chest, creating the most soothing sensations. "Your son and the gargoyle met us at the hospital. Once the EMTs had taken X-rays and set your leg, we smuggled you out." Teasing his fingertips over Albert's nipple, Spieron added, "Even though our bond is incomplete, answering questions about blood work will still be tough. I might have to alter their memories."

Albert hummed as he nodded. With Spieron's hands on him, tracing over his torso, his body had a predictable reaction. His blood heated, and while sluggish, it still began to flow into his prick.

Spieron groaned softly as he nuzzled Albert's neck. "Oh, my beloved love," he mumbled roughly. "We can't do what your body is calling us to do."

Chuckling roughly, Albert mumbled, "I know, but I can't help my response to you." He sighed as he turned his head and nuzzled into Spieron's soft auburn hair. "I know you don't wear cologne, but you smell so damn good."

When Spieron sighed deeply, Albert sluggishly realized what he'd said. He smiled absently. "How long am I laid up for?" Then he realized he hadn't received an answer about his horses. "And my geldings?"

"Good idea," Spieron murmured. "Talk about something else until you pass out." He pressed his lips to Albert's neck, causing goose bumps to rise on his skin. "While waiting for the helicopter, I unsaddled your boys and put them in the paddock. A friend is going to see after them until Nicholas's trailer gets there in a couple of days."

"Trailer?"

Oh, I'm parroting my vampire. I must be ready to pass out again.

Spieron chuckled as he nuzzled him. "Don't fight your need for sleep, Albert," he crooned, his words telling Albert that he'd spoken out loud.

Damn.

"You won't be able to go back to the cabin for a while," Spieron told him, his voice quiet, soft and soothing. "It was a bad break. You're gonna need help for at least a month." Nibbling at his neck, Spieron admitted, "We can discuss where we want to live after that."

Fatigue overtaking him—or maybe that was the meds—Albert grunted his understanding.

After that, he didn't remember much.

CHAPTER NINE

Spieron heard Albert coming before scenting him. The *scuff thump, scuff thump* of his lover's slipper-clad foot hitting hardwood alternating between crutches gave away his approach. Rising from the chair where he sat on the porch, Spieron crossed to the back door and opened it.

Smiling at his frowning beloved, Spieron could guess at what bothered the male. He bit back his instinct to offer a hand to help. Opening the door ruffled his man's feathers enough.

My poor dominant human.

"Hi, beloved," Spieron greeted, stepping backward while holding the door. "Come enjoy the sunshine with me."

"I feel so fucking lazy," Albert grumbled as he exited the house. "I haven't done anything constructive for over a month."

"Well, I have some good news, if you're interested in exercise," Spieron stated, releasing the screen door and allowing it to swing shut. "Come have a seat with me, and I'll tell you all about it."

"How about you tell me while we take a stroll to the barn," Albert countered, his bearded lips pressed into a hard line. "I've been on my ass and back enough these past few weeks to last me a lifetime."

Spieron nodded as he noticed that Albert wasn't wearing a slipper on his good foot after all. Instead, he'd donned the slip-on *Dockers* Spieron had bought him as soon as his lover had been cleared for clutches. It had taken ten days, since

Albert's left thigh had been bruised and sore from his horse's hoof-strike.

Good thing my man didn't break both legs. I can't imagine how angry he would have been to land in a wheelchair.

Feeling grateful to the gods for small favors — *my beloved is alive and well at my side* — Spieron trotted down the three steps that led to the dirt ground. He paused and turned, watching carefully as his lover made his way down them. His fingers twitched with his desire to assist, but once again, he beat it back.

"I ain't gonna fall," Albert grumbled, flashing a scowl Spieron's way. Then he grimaced and muttered, "Sorry. Damn, I don't meanta snap."

"You're way out of your element, my beloved," Spieron offered, falling into step beside Albert as he began moving across the yard toward the main barn. "No one likes being injured."

"Or horny as hell but can't do much about it." Albert's cheeks took on a pinkish hue under his beard, but he still added, "As much as I appreciate your hands and mouth, Spieron, I want in your ass so fuckin' bad."

Spieron barked a laugh as he listened to his human whine.

"Shut up," Albert griped. "It ain't funny."

Reaching out, Spieron teased his fingertips up and down Albert's spine. He couldn't take his human's hand with him being on crutches, but he still needed to touch. His desire to confirm that his beloved was truly there and at his side would make him do no less.

It helped that the move seemed to settle and relax Albert, for his lover sighed deeply and even managed to bump his upper arm into Spieron.

"And with that opening, that news I have to tell you may bring a smile to your face," Spieron stated, then took a quick look around and lowered his voice. "Melissa will be here on

Friday to check your leg. Maybe change out your cast to something smaller."

Currently, due to the complexity of the fracture of his fibula, Albert had been forced to wear a cast from above his knee all the way down to his foot. The doctors had feared that any rotation of either ankle or knee would pull the healing bones apart. While the human doctors had talked of having Albert in the cast for eight weeks before checking, because Spieron and Albert had already started their bond, Melissa had anticipated that his healing might have already begun to speed up.

Spieron was damned hopeful that she was right.

"Oh, yeah?" Albert immediately perked up, a hopeful smile tugging at his whiskered cheeks. "That'd be great."

"And if that is the case"—Spieron waggled his brows as he winked at Albert—"you'll have more mobility."

The growl that Albert let out sent a fissure of heat through Spieron's veins.

Gods, this man does it for me.

Grinning, Spieron rubbed Albert's lower back, then skimmed his hand down farther. "Actually, I was thinking"—he rubbed over his lover's ass before cupping one cheek and squeezing lightly—"that after I ride your dick into submission, I'll open you up and fill you with my seed."

Albert froze, almost stumbling on his crutches.

Spieron grabbed his upper arm, steadying him. Offering his beloved a wry smile, he murmured, "Sorry. Maybe I shouldn't have sprung that on you like that."

Rasping out a low chuckle, Albert grinned, and his eyes twinkled. "Oh, that isn't the only thing that sprung." He glanced pointedly at his own groin before once again meeting Spieron's gaze. "And I can't wait to enjoy everything you mentioned."

Spieron felt an answering surge of desire upon seeing Albert's response to his comments, not to mention his oh-so-pleasant scent. "Oh, Albert," he purred as he stepped in front of his beloved. Gripping his waist with one hand, he cradled his bearded jaw with the other. "I—"

"Hey, Dad! Glad to see you out and about!"

Nicholas's hollered words stalled Spieron's murmured promises . . . which was probably a good thing. They *were* standing in the middle of the yard, after all. Turning to face Nicholas, Spieron couldn't help but notice Albert's proud grin.

After Albert and Spieron had moved in and gotten settled, the four of them—Albert, Spieron, Nicholas, and Bodb—had discussed the pros and cons of perpetuating the secret of Nicholas and Albert's true relationship. They'd even brought in the ranch foreman—Stanley Redfeather. After a week of Stanley feeling out the ranch hands for where their loyalties laid, not to mention Bodb sharing the background checks he'd had run on everyone, they'd come to a decision.

While Nicholas had been surprised that Bodb had information on all his employees, Spieron had understood. As a gargoyle elder, the male needed to know who was around him on a regular basis. Bodb had a number of enforcers in the area, too.

Lebone was a mated gargoyle with a fox shifter wife who did the cooking—Pauline. He'd been hired on as a wrangler. Spieron had caught the scent of Biscane, an unmated gargoyle, every now and again when he'd gone on evening walks. There were two others as well. One was Sindrid, a mated gargoyle with a male human mate, who was handy with plants and had started a garden. The final male was also an unmated enforcer—Ssimeas—and he was often scarce, too.

Finally, the decision had been made to sit all the hands down and explain the relationship. They'd asked for their discretion. Each man—and the two female wranglers—had been sworn to secrecy.

As far as Spieron had been able to tell, everyone had been telling the truth when they vowed to keep the information under their *Stetsons*—their words.

"Hey, son," Albert called back. "Yeah, tired of bein' stuck in the house."

Nicholas jogged the short distance across the yard, joining them. As soon as he reached them, he wrapped Albert in a one-armed hug. Just as quickly, he stepped away, and they all once again started toward the barn.

"Are you out here to meet Jasper?" Nicholas asked.

"Uh, no." Albert's brows furrowed in confusion. "Who's that?"

Nicholas snorted. "Our newest quarter horse foal. We might keep this little guy a stud. He's going to be gorgeous, I bet." Then Nicholas whistled and added, "And the way he moves. Day-am! So cowy."

"Nice! Let's check him out," Albert responded with a grin.

Spieron followed the pair as they talked horses, relief filling him. For the first time in weeks, his lover was finally showing an interest in something. Well, something other than sex, but they couldn't do that all the time.

Laughing at his thoughts, Spieron found himself looking forward to meeting the little stud colt.

"Boss, you in here?"

Spieron watched Albert open his mouth, then snap it closed again.

At the same time, Nicholas called, "Yeah, Stanley. What'd ya need?" Even as he spoke, he unhaltered the colt he'd been handling.

While Spieron didn't know anything about raising horses,

he thought the little one was surprisingly calm and friendly. The colt had walked up to Nicholas in the stall and had easily accepted a halter. While he'd stood stock-still and stared wide-eyed and with his ears pricked forward when Albert had hobbled into the stall, he hadn't tried to yank away.

Spieron figured those were all good marks for his temperament.

"Looks like your brother's car is comin' down the drive," Stanley told him once he was close enough that he didn't have to shout. "Seems someone is with him. Maybe your mom?"

"Vernon is here?" Nicholas exited the stall, carefully locking the door behind him. "Was he expected, and I forgot?"

"No, sir," Stanley replied, rubbing the day or two worth of scruff on his jaw. "Nothing on the ranch schedule."

"Yeah, it was a dumb question," Nicholas grumbled as he began heading down the aisle. He paused and waited for Albert to catch up. Spieron stayed right beside him. Nicholas lifted a brow. "If you don't want to deal with family, you don't have to."

Albert shrugged, although a fresh set of tension sat between his shoulders. "I'm gonna have to face 'em sometime." After catching Spieron's gaze, he stated, "Why don't we go sit on the back porch. I could use a glass of sweet tea."

Spieron understood. Albert wanted the first time he saw his estranged nephew and ex-lover in a comfortable setting.

"Sounds good to me," Spieron replied. "Although I'll take a lemonade."

"I still can't figure out how you can enjoy that bitter drink," Albert countered, although he smiled a bit as he spoke. "And you still taste like sweet red licorice."

It was a common argument, and Spieron knew Albert did it to calm his nerves. As a vampire, he could not only scent his lover's unease, but he could hear the race of his pulse through his veins. Even as it called to him, for him to take a sip and enjoy Albert's delicious life-blood, Spieron hoped to help calm his man, too.

"I'll bring 'em round as long as Vernon is going to be civil," Nicholas stated around a growl.

From what Spieron had surmised whenever he'd heard Nicholas talk about Vernon, he and his brother—or half-brother, considering—had just as tense a relationship as Albert and Baltus did.

"Sounds good," Spieron replied, then rested his palm against Albert's lower back.

After separating at the doors of the barn—Nicholas and Stanley striding swiftly across the yard toward the front of the house—Spieron and Albert started toward the back. When the other pair was out of earshot, Albert glanced his way with one eyebrow lifted. "Proprietary much?"

Spieron scoffed when he realized his move could definitely be read that way. "Yep." He wasn't going to lie. Knowing he needed to explain, Spieron admitted, "I may end up meeting your ex-lover, Nicholas's mother, and our bond is not secure." Grimacing, he told him, "I'm feeling a little possessive. I'm gonna have to ask you to deal with it, because I'm not certain how much of the sensation I can curb."

Having reached the base of the steps, Albert paused. He balanced awkwardly on one crutch as he rested the second against the railing. Then Albert turned and reached out, gripping Spieron's jaw.

Nuzzling into his lover's hold, Spieron gripped his upper arm, offering support.

"Come 'ere," Albert rumbled, using his hold to tug ever-so-lightly.

"I'm here," Spieron countered as he smiled and took that last step between them.

"Then kiss me, goddammit," Albert insisted gruffly. His eyes narrowed. "No matter who's around. This is our home, and I ain't hidin' ya. Not from anyone."

For an instant, Spieron couldn't believe what he'd just heard. He couldn't help it. A wide grin split his lips, and his heart tripped wildly in his chest.

Spieron was more than happy to take Albert up on that offer. He tightened his hand on Albert's upper arm as he slipped his other around his lover's waist. Tipping his head, he met Albert's lips. His beloved instantly opened to him, and Spieron took advantage.

Normally, Albert quickly took control. This time, however, he allowed Spieron to direct the kiss. Relishing the opportunity, he slowly explored his man's mouth, dipping his tongue in deep and enjoying Albert's masculine flavor.

As was typical, any time Spieron touched Albert in any way other than platonic—and even sometimes then, too—his body fired to life. His blood flowed south, and his dick thickened. Spieron groaned roughly as he pressed closer, wanting to feel his lover's body against his own.

Except, that move knocked Albert off balance.

Spieron felt his beloved snap his head up and release his neck and jaw. He saw his man's arm pinwheel and figured out his problem damn fast. Hissing a curse under his breath, Spieron tightened his hold and pulled Albert back toward him, helping set him to rights.

Albert's deep chuckles flooded Spieron with relief. His man wasn't upset. In fact, Albert winked at him as he grinned. The crinkles at the corners of Albert's eyes betrayed true happiness even as he grabbed his second crutch and positioned it under his arm.

"Sorry about that," Spieron couldn't help but say even as he helped Albert up the steps.

The fact that Albert didn't complain about the assistance

proved exactly how happy he was. "Don't worry about it. I asked ya to kiss me, and we always seem to get carried away." As he turned right and headed toward the covered deck area, Albert flashed a grin Spieron's way before adding huskily, "And I love that about us."

Then Albert thumped his way to a hanging rocking chair and settled onto one side of it. He patted the space next to him before resting his crutches against the nearby end table. Crossing to Albert, Spieron grabbed a footstool that was also a gliding rocker style, and he helped Albert lift his casted leg onto it and get comfortable.

Then Spieron obeyed his man, and he eased onto the rocking bench beside him. Albert slung his arm over the back and rested his thick fingers around Spieron's nape. The hold was just as possessive as the one he'd had on his lover as they'd crossed the yard, and Spieron's heart raced.

He fucking loved it.

As a vampire, Spieron had always thought he would end up the more dominant in his relationship with his beloved. He had quickly learned that with Albert, that wasn't the case. His man needed to be in control, and it was these little actions that allowed Spieron to give that to his beloved, to fulfill his human's needs.

Albert sighed deeply as he focused a loving look on Spieron. "You spoil me, you know."

Spieron shook his head. "Nope." Resting his hand on Albert's thigh, he squeezed lightly. "Just taking care of my man. That's all."

"Love it," Albert stated gruffly. "Love you."

Then Albert again used his hold to pull Spieron toward him.

Spieron's heart rate spiked. He never tired of hearing his human tell him that. It helped settle his vampire nature, the part of him that desperately wanted to complete their bond even though Spieron knew they had to wait until Albert was given the all clear to do so.

Just before their lips met, a dry voice full of disdain stated, "So, you *are* here . . . and you're a fag."

Turning his head, Spieron scowled at the intruder. He recognized the lean, toned, dirty-blond-haired man as Vernon. Not only had he seen pictures, but the son had been in Baltus's memories.

"Vernon," Albert stated evenly. "That's not a very nice thing to say, and I consider myself bisexual, but seeing as Spieron is my partner, I can understand your mistake."

Curling his lip, Vernon glanced between them. "First Mitch. Then Nicholas. Now you?" He sneered as he shook his head. "I woulda thought it was something in the water or maybe like father like son if it weren't for Mitch having found his partner in Colorado."

Albert's brows shot up, and Spieron realized he'd also caught on to Vernon's meaning.

Vernon must have realized it, too. "Oh, yeah. I know you're Nick's father." Scoffing, he rolled his eyes. "Mom's pretty. So I get it." Then he smirked as he met Spieron's gaze. "Better not get your heart too invested, man. Uncle Albert's a cheater." His smile turned cruel as he said in a sing-song voice, "Once a cheater, always a cheater."

Only Albert's hand on his neck stayed Spieron's instinct to spring up and smack the young asshole.

"If you don't have anything nice to say," Albert stated evenly. "Please leave."

"Oh, I will in a minute," Vernon replied glibly.

His dark-brown eyes held a malicious gleam that reminded Spieron of his father. His next words confirmed that the apple hadn't fallen far from the tree.

"I just swung by to deliver an eviction notice to Nicholas." Vernon chuckled coldly. "Don't get too comfortable here, Uncle, because this isn't Nick's place to welcome you. Ya'll have seventy-two hours to get your shit together and get off my ranch."

CHAPTER TEN

A lbert felt his chest tighten, and he suddenly found it hard to breathe. After all this time, all the sacrifices he'd made so this wouldn't happen, it was still coming to pass? His son was losing the ranch?

"Out of curiosity, Vernon, why are you doing this?"

Spieron's calm tone drew Albert out of his panic-induced haze.

Turning his attention on his lover, Albert realized that Spieron appeared relaxed, too. His left brow was arched, and his chin was tipped up, almost making it appear he was looking down his nose at Vernon. A nice trick, considering the vampire was seated.

Vernon leveled a cold gaze Spieron's way. "Why do you think? Money." His face morphed into an innocent expression. "This is my birthright, being the firstborn male to Father, so of course I'm going to make certain it remains in our hands." Then he shrugged, but his expression of nonchalance wasn't fooling anyone. "Besides, since Nick is a fag, it's not like he can produce an heir to take over the ranch when he gets older. This is the perfect solution."

That statement caused something to click in Albert's mind. "Sandra," he whispered. After clearing his throat, he stated louder, "Have you spoken about Nicholas's relationship with Sandra's father?"

Finally, Vernon's expression cleared for real, and a hint of the kind, fun-loving teenager he'd once been showed through. "No." Crossing his arms over his chest, Vernon peered left toward the horse paddocks. "I couldn't really give a shit that Nicholas is gay." He focused on Albert. "Or you, Uncle."

"Bisexual," Albert corrected softly. Squeezing Spieron's neck where he still gripped his nape, he gave his vampire a warm smile. "And good. Because love is love."

"Well, yeah," Vernon muttered, sounding uncomfortable.

The way Vernon rocked back on his feet returned Albert's attention to his nephew. For just an instant, the twenty-six-year-old lawyer appeared almost . . . lost. The expression cleared swiftly enough, and Vernon once again stared coldly at them.

Unable to reconcile the two sides, Albert blurted out, "Vernon, why are you really doing this?"

Vernon scoffed, rolling his eyes. "I told you. Money." Then he started toward the back door but paused and peered back at Albert. His lips pressed into a hard line. "When Mom heard you were here with a man, she refused to come see you. She disowned Nick. That's how I found out about—" Vernon paused, waving his hand between them. "She helped me start the paperwork. Said it was what Dad would have wanted."

Then Vernon stalked away, his body rigid with obvious tension.

Spieron blew out a long breath, then turned and met Albert's gaze. "I couldn't influence Vernon's mind." He sounded damn surprised. "That's rare."

"How rare? And what do you mean?" Albert hadn't even realized that Spieron had been trying to see into Vernon's mind. Was there a way to tell?

"Vampires can influence most humans with their trancing ability," Spieron explained. "It's what allows us to feed from a partner without them realizing it. All they remember is that they had a very good time." The smirk his words had generated faded from his lips, and his eyes narrowed as his expression turned vacant. "The other one percent cannot be influenced. It's extremely rare." Spieron hummed. "I could influence his father . . . so why not him?"

"So what are we going to do?" Albert asked. "If Katrina hates me so much because I hooked up with a man"—he paused and shook his head—"well, she learned to be vindictive and manipulative from the best."

Spieron nodded. "Baltus. Right."

He opened his mouth, but the squeak of the screen door's hinges drew both men's attention, and he snapped his mouth shut again.

Bodb was guiding a clearly shell-shocked Nicholas with one hand. In his other, he carried a tray of drinks. His expression appeared grim, and lines of tension radiated from his clenched jaw.

After seeing Nicholas to a large lounge chair, Bodb held the tray out toward them. Spieron leaned forward and grabbed a pair of glasses, one clearly sweet tea and the other lemonade. As Bodb placed the tray on a center table, then handed another glass of tea to Nicholas, Albert took his own tea from Spieron.

Once Bodb had slipped behind Nicholas on the lounge chair, bracketing his lover with his thighs and with his arm around his waist, Nicholas leaned back against his gargoyle and let out a long sigh.

Bodb glanced between them. "Did Vernon tell you what he and his lawyer were doing here?"

"He did," Albert acknowledged softly. "I think it's an attack on me from Katrina, and I think she's using Vernon, and Nicholas is caught in the middle."

"Of course the lawyer was here, too," Spieron mused absently. "I was so caught up trying to penetrate Vernon's mind that I didn't consider I might be able to get what we needed from him." He dipped his head and shrugged. "At least, some of what we needed."

"You couldn't influence Vernon?" Bodb seemed surprised by that, too.

Spieron shook his head.

Bodb hummed, then smirked. "Aren't there a couple of demons living in your coven?"

Scoffing, Spieron nodded. "There are. Two. Toni's beloved, Abyzou, as well as Balthazar. He's bonded with a donor who grew up a ward of our coven, so both are considered members until they choose to leave."

"Wait a minute. Demons?" Albert gaped as he met Nicholas's gaze. "Did you know about these demons?"

"I'd heard of demons but haven't met any," Nicholas admitted. Lifting his hand in placation, he added, "From what I understand, they're not inherently evil like religions tote. Instead, they work for the Four Horsemen of the Apocalypse." Nicholas glanced at Spieron, then over his shoulder at Bodb. "Did I get that right?"

Spieron hummed as he nodded, squeezing Albert's thigh to draw his attention. "The tasks they do help the world and those living in this plane stay in balance."

Albert nodded, deciding he was going to dwell on all that another time. Instead, he focused on Bodb and asked, "How could they help?"

Bodb rubbed over Nicholas's stomach lightly as he rumbled, "Demon magick is different than a vampire's trancing ability. It affects not only all humans, but they can even manipulate the weak-minded paranormal." He turned his attention back to Spieron. "Think one of them would be willing to come and look into the minds of Nicholas and Albert's family? See if we can figure out their true motives?"

Spieron hummed for a second, his brows furrowing. He even took a drink of his lemonade, clearly stalling. "We could ask, but they would have to get permission from whichever horseman they serve. Their allegiance isn't truly to the coven, it's to their *amina*, their soul-bonded one, so Master Adalric can't order them." Grimacing, Spieron admitted, "They should be considered a last resort."

Bodb nodded. "Okay."

"I never suspected Mom was a bigot," Nicholas whispered. He stared vacantly into his tea, and Albert wondered if his son had even registered the last few minutes of conversation. Then Nicholas snapped his attention up, and his eyes widened. "Sandra! What if she tells Sandra's father? He'll disinherit her. She—"

"Nick?"

Everyone turned to see both Sandra and Maggie standing just inside the screen door. The women peered out at them. Their fingers were twined, and both sported creased brows and worried expressions.

"Hey, Sandra," Nicholas greeted. After a glance around at the group, he beckoned. "Better come sit. This concerns you and Maggie, too."

"I'll get us some tea," Maggie whispered before slipping away.

Sandra joined them on the porch, glancing around at everyone. "I saw Vernon come by with a guy in a suit." She settled on a rocking chair similar to the one Albert and Spieron gently swayed in. "Is this about . . . us?" Sandra gave Nicholas a pointed look.

Nicholas heaved a sigh even as he rubbed his free hand over Bodb's wrist where it rested on his stomach.

Albert bet his son was taking comfort from his gargoyle, the same as Spieron's hand on his thigh and how he touched his vampire's neck bolstered his own confidence.

"I'm afraid so," Nicholas admitted. "We made the decision not to hide our true relationships at home, remember?"

Sandra nodded even as her gaze strayed to the squeaking door which heralded Maggie's reappearance.

Seeing that she carried a lemonade as well as sweet tea, Albert smiled. His vampire had corrupted Maggie. He silently chuckled at his thoughts as Sandra took the tea and Maggie settled next to her.

The women immediately held hands.

"Did I miss much?" Maggie murmured, glancing around the group before taking a sip of her drink.

Nicholas shook his head. "Uh, should we tell them everything?" Albert watched as the women exchanged a confused glance, but Nicholas kept talking. "I mean, if we're going to use paranormal means to keep them safe, then—" He paused and shrugged.

Bodb nodded. "They live here. They should know what's going on in their home, but I don't want to tell the hands." A low growl erupted from them as he added, "One of them had to have shared something of what's going on around here, even if it was just a comment in the wrong place with the wrong people."

"Agreed," Spieron instantly replied. He met Albert's gaze. "I'd like to know which one of them ran their mouth, so Katrina found out about us." Leaning closer to him, Spieron's deep green eyes held a heated gleam. "You know we're not hiding. You are my beloved, my everything, but we do need to know who we can trust."

Albert immediately nodded, understanding. "If he said something about our relationship, he could have said something about Nicholas, too."

"Exactly," Spieron whispered before closing the distance between them.

When Spieron's lips met his own, Albert tightened his hand on his lover's neck. He rubbed along the edge of his jawline, urging his lover to tilt his head a little. Just like every time Albert kissed Spieron, his vampire gave in to his lead, and a heady rush of power surged through him.

Albert pushed his tongue into Spieron's mouth, licking, lapping, and enjoying his man's taste.

Damn. How does he always taste like red licorice bites?

"Guys, could we finish here?" Bodb asked loudly, although amusement filled his tone.

At the same time, a feminine giggle reached his ears at the same time as a soft sigh followed by, "Ahhhh."

After bringing their kiss to an end, Albert pecked Spieron's lips, then grinned. "You always make me forget myself."

Spieron smiled back, his green eyes dark, betraying his desire. "Should I apologize?"

"Never." Albert pecked Spieron's lips again, then straightened, and his vampire did the same.

My vampire. Hell yeah.

Albert liked how that sounded in his mind, and he shifted in his seat as he thought about completing their bond.

"So, uh . . . I'm almost afraid to ask," Sandra stated, brushing a stray wisp of blonde hair from her face and tucking it behind her ear. Then she took Maggie's hand again. "What do you mean by paranormal?"

Maggie's brown eyes lit up, and she leaned forward in her seat. "Oooo, do you mean like ghosts and spirits and demons and stuff?"

Albert hid his surprise by taking a swig of his sweet tea. Spieron and Bodb exchanged glances. It was Nicholas who answered.

"Well, demons, sure. Eventually, anyway," Nicholas began slowly. "Wait. Do you know something about demons?" Waving his hand as if to wipe away his question, Nicholas hurriedly said, "Never mind. Um. What we need to explain was that things like vampires and shifters and gargoyles are real, and they live right here on earth with us."

To everyone's surprise, Sandra and Maggie exchanged a look. Then Maggie's smile turned smug as she swept her gaze over the men. "We already know that."

"I know it's hard to believe, but—" Nicholas paused, obviously not having expected that. "Wait. What? How do you know?"

Sandra giggled, bumping her shoulder into Maggie's.

Maggie continued to grin as she focused on Bodb, "Well, you should tell your hulking, dark-blue friend that he's not nearly as good at hiding in the shadows as he thinks he is."

Laughing again, Sandra added, "But he's better than the huge black one." She winked at Nicholas and Bodb. "We hardly ever see him."

Bodb barked a laugh, his lips parting in surprise. As he shook his head, his amusement gleamed in his brown eyes. "The blue male is Ssimeas. The black one is Biscane."

Still smiling, Maggie commented, "Well, it's nice to have names to go with their faces."

"Why didn't you freak out or ask about them?" Albert certainly knew he would have.

Maggie sobered, then exchanged another look with Sandra. Nicholas's wife nodded encouragingly. "I knew what they were because I'm a witch." Shrugging her slender shoulders, she cleared her throat, then focused on Bodb. "I figured they were your bodyguards." Then her face turned beet red. "Because we saw you change once, too."

"Shit," Bodb muttered. "Where was that? When?"

"Two days after we moved in," Sandra told him. "We were taking an evening ride near the west pond, and you were out there talking with the black gargoyle." She hesitated a second, then snapped her fingers. "Um, Biscane."

Maggie nodded in agreement. Then she focused on Spieron. "But I don't know what you are. What's your secret?"

"I'm a vampire," Spieron replied easily. Then he winked.

"But don't worry. The only one I bite"—he turned a heated gaze on Albert—"is my beloved."

"Well, now that we're all on the same page with the paranormal," Nicholas began with amusement.

Sandra waved her drink. "Oh, no. I have so many questions for you guys," she said, waggling her finger between Bodb and Spieron.

"Later," Bodb countered. To soften his refusal, he added, "We'll both answer anything"—Spieron nodded, too—"but right now, we have a problem with Nicholas's family." Bodb growled softly as he glared at nothing, although Albert noticed his arm muscles bulged as if he were clutching Nicholas tighter to his chest. At the same time, Bodb dipped his head a little and muttered, "I'm getting damn tired of your family's meddling, my mate."

"Me, too," Nicholas instantly replied.

Over the next hour, Nicholas and Bodb told how they'd originally dealt with Baltus. The women listened, and Sandra once more apologized for getting Nicholas into their mess. Nicholas waved away her comments, telling her he would do it again.

They also learned that Sandra was Maggie's equivalent of a mate or beloved, although as a witch, she referred to her as her familiar. A witch connected with that person's lifethread, giving her more stability so they could create more powerful spells. A familiar also kept a witch from burning out from the power they commanded, so the pair lived longer.

Maggie told them that her grandmother, Lidia, a powerful practitioner, was still alive and well at the age of one-hundred-eighty-seven, living happily with her familiar, Maggie's grandfather, Artie. Once Lidia had discovered that Maggie presented as a witch at puberty, Maggie had lived for almost three decades with her grandmother, learning her craft. Albert thought Maggie looked fantastic at age sixty-three. She didn't look a day over twenty-five.

"So . . . the answer as far as our problems is simple, in my opinion," Sandra stated suddenly, straightening in her seat. "It's time I tell my father the truth. On my terms." Meeting Maggie's gaze, she murmured, "And then we'll probably have to move, because I don't think we can find jobs here with all the influence the Kartwright family wields."

Nicholas immediately shook his head. "As long as this ranch is under my control, you and Maggie will always have a home here." He smiled at the pair. "You're family."

"Well, then, we need to figure out a way to keep this ranch in your hands." Spieron grinned as he glanced around the group. "And I actually have an idea about that." He curved his lips into a wry smile. "As long as a few of us don't mind doing something a little uncomfortable."

Chapter Eleven

Even though Spieron knew it was his plan, he really didn't want to do it. Feeling uncomfortable was an understatement, and from the scents pouring off Albert, Spieron knew his beloved wasn't feeling much better. He figured part of the reason was that this was the first time he'd been off the ranch since his injury, so Albert couldn't be all that comfortable with his big, heavy cast.

Spieron wished they could have waited until after Melissa visited. Not only would Albert have had more mobility, but they would have been able to complete their bond. Unfortunately, with only a quickly dwindling seventy-two-hour window, they couldn't wait.

That was why, while Nicholas, Bodb, Maggie, and Sandra were arriving unannounced at Sandra's father's office to discuss Nicholas and Sandra's annulment, Albert and Spieron were headed to Katrina's townhome. Word had it that she was there hosting an early luncheon. Their plan would work better with an audience.

"Ready to do this?" Spieron asked as he parked his truck. He was grateful to have his wheels back, even if he would never admit that to anyone. When Spieron didn't receive a response, he reached over and gripped Albert's thigh and rubbed lightly. That drew his beloved's attention, and he smiled at Albert. "You ready?"

Albert blew out a breath, then shook his head. "Not really, no." A hard glimmer entered his brown eyes. "But I'm gonna do it . . . for family."

"For family," Spieron confirmed, nodding.

After one more nod, Albert cleared his throat, then reached for the door handle.

Spieron made quick work of exiting his truck, shutting the door, and zipping around to the other side. Gripping Albert's upper arm in a loose hold, he helped his beloved from his truck. After Spieron opened the back door and grabbed his lover's crutches, he handed them to Albert.

Albert sighed deeply as he fitted them under his armpits. After a quick smile, his mountain man hobbled out of the way. Spieron closed both doors and locked his vehicle before falling into step with Albert, meeting his slow pace.

"Why am I not surprised that Katrina lives in a gated community," Spieron commented quietly as he peered around the area. He tapped his phone a couple of times, then slid it into the chest pocket of the polo shirt he wore. "Good thing Nicholas remembered the code."

Smirking, Albert teased, "Are you saying one of your coven's tech guys couldn't have figured it out?"

Spieron winked, his tension easing upon hearing Albert's bit of mirth. "Could have, but it might have taken longer than we wanted." Brushing Albert's lower back with his hand, he glanced around the large parking area. "Recognize any of the cars?"

Albert shook his head. "These are the kind of people that replace their vehicle every two or three years with a new, better, fancier model," he explained, snorting. "Waste of money, in my opinion."

Humming, Spieron nodded. "Agreed, but at least it gives us an idea of a head count." Even though he had no desire to shell out the excess cash to own one of the fancy vehicles, Spieron still admired them. "Six guests. Unless you think someone carpooled?"

Barking a laugh, Spieron watched deep laugh lines crease

around his beloved's eyes. "Not a chance," he said around his amusement.

"Well, let's do this," Spieron muttered when they reached the door. As he rang the bell, never had he wanted to see someone less than he did Albert's ex. Still, for family, Spieron would get this done.

The door opened, and a butler peered out at him. The middle-aged gentleman couldn't hide his surprise upon seeing Albert there. He hesitated, giving Albert the opening he needed.

"Afternoon, Simon," Albert greeted even as he took a lurching step forward. "It's good to see you. How is Meredith?"

Spieron guessed that was a wife.

"She is well, sir," Simon replied, his expression appearing uncertain. He took a step backward, swinging the door wider.

Sometimes an injury could come in handy.

"She's a senior this year, isn't she?" Albert continued the conversation as if he spoke with the butler on a regular basis and everything was completely normal. "Has she chosen any colleges?"

Oh. A daughter then.

Simon glanced between them as Spieron followed close behind Albert. His mouth opened once, twice, then he replied, "Yes, sir. She's been accepted into MIT."

"Well, damn, man." Albert paused, carefully balanced on his foot and one crutch, and used the hand he'd freed to pat Simon on the shoulder. "You must be proud. That's amazing!"

"Yes, sir. Very proud," Simon replied, sounding a bit confused. Perhaps it was the tap of Albert's crutches on the marble foyer that yanked the butler from his daze, for he swiftly closed the door and hurried after them. "I'm sorry, sir, but Madam Lindson didn't tell me you were coming. Are you expected?"

Albert grinned as he shook his head. "Naw, but we won't interrupt her luncheon for long. Five minutes, I'm sure." He winked, doing a damn good job at appearing good-natured and relaxed. "Don't worry. I know the way."

"I should really announce you, sir," Simon countered, although he made no move to actually stop Albert. "And your companion, sir? Perhaps you'd like to wait in the salon? I could have Tabatha bring you some sweet tea."

Once more, Spieron appreciated the fact that Albert was injured—not that he ever wanted his beloved in pain, but the cast and crutches made a fantastic deterrent.

"I'll just be in and out, Simon," Albert assured, flashing another grin the butler's way. "I happened to be in town, you see, on my way to do a couple of other errands. I won't be long."

By then they'd reached a large, arched opening off to the right of the hallway. Spieron had been cognizant of the buzz of conversation, but he hadn't paid attention to it. He'd been too focused on Albert, Simon, and making certain the butler didn't attempt to stop or injure his beloved in any way.

Albert rounded the corner as if he owned the place, a big grin on his face—he'd even trimmed his beard for the occasion, shaving off the bushy whiskers. Spieron was damn pleased his beloved hadn't gotten rid of all of it, but he did like the more clean-cut look, too. Now his facial hair accentuated his underlying bone structure. On top of that, Albert wore a nice pair of jeans—one leg split and tied around the cast with leather laces to accommodate the cast—as well as a dark-blue button-downed shirt.

My mountain man cleans up damn nice.

"Good morning, Katrina," Albert greeted. Pausing and balancing, he lifted his hand and tipped his hat toward the six other ladies seated at the table. "Ladies. My apologies for interrupting. I won't be long."

Ever-so-slowly, her body stiff and with a cool smile curving her painted lips, the woman at the head of the table rose from her seat. "Albert. I didn't expect you." Her gaze shifted to Spieron, and her smile turned brittle. "And you are?"

Spieron just managed to bite back his smirk. *No time like the present.* "You know who I am, Katrina." Then, curving his lips into a charming smile as he swept his attention over the other ladies, Spieron stated, "But for those who don't know me. I'm Spieron Virche." He rested his palm on his chest and gave a half-bow before straightening. "I am Albert's partner, and the catalyst Katrina needed to encourage her sons to fight for the deed of the ranch."

Upon hearing the soft gasps of several of the women around the room, Spieron returned his focus to Katrina. The red tint to her cheeks told him that he was getting under her skin, so he continued. "Of course, poor Vernon probably couldn't care less about being the heir to the ranch. He's happiest behind a desk. That much is obvious."

Too bad Spieron couldn't grin widely, but that could cause other problems. Instead, he winked at Katrina and returned his focus to the half dozen ladies as he shoved his hands into his pockets. "Sadly, Vernon wants to please his mother, so he's doing his best to disrupt the lives of all those living at a very prosperous cattle ranch that he doesn't actually want to have anything to do with." Spieron heaved a put upon sigh before finishing, "Kinda sad. Right?"

"I think you have spouted enough lies for this morning," Katrina stated coldly. "Leave now before I have Simon call the police."

If looks could kill, Spieron knew he would be dead.

"Won't even call the police yourself?" Spieron focused his attention on her mind. "I really think you need to tell your friends why you suddenly hate Nicholas so much." To Spieron's pleasure, he felt the mental link form in his mind that told him he had gained control of another's thoughts. "Why do you hate Nicholas?"

"Because of him!" Katrina screamed, pointing at Albert. "He's a faggot! A pervert! And still, he seduced me." As her screeching words filled the dining room, several women gasped, but Katrina kept going. "Nicholas is a bastard! He shouldn't get the ranch. It should stay in Baltus's line. He's a real man! He knows how to make money, to offer a comfortable life for his wife." Katrina turned hate-filled eyes on Albert. "And you're just a glorified cowboy that was fun to slum with."

By the time Katrina finished her rant, all the women's eyes were wide. A couple of them had their hands over their mouths, obviously attempting to hide their shock. One woman was even slack-jawed.

"Times are changing, Katrina," Albert responded quietly. "I never realized you had so much hate inside you. I'm sorry you're passing it on to Vernon." Smiling calmly, he swept his gaze over all the women. "I apologize for interrupting your gathering. I had only hoped to ask why Vernon decided to show up at the ranch and attempt to evict Nicholas without warning." Sighing deeply, Albert focused back on Katrina. "Now I understand. You told him it was Baltus who had changed his will before his riding accident. Did you forge the paperwork? Or did Baltus write it up years ago and you found it and decided to use it for your own gain? Or maybe you forged it?"

Still under Spieron's compulsion, with just a little push from him, he had Katrina answering truthfully.

Scoffing, Katrina replied, "I found something similar in Baltus's files, but it was too old to submit. The terminology was expired." She smirked, her expression turning smug. "But it gave me ideas. You probably thought I was just some dumb socialite, but I've paid attention over the years. It was simple to alter the document and use it to convince Vernon that the ranch should be his." Sighing deeply, Katrina simpered, "He always was the best son. So eager to please. He'll do anything to make his mommy happy."

The women at the table were glancing between each other. They obviously couldn't believe what they'd just heard Katrina admit to. Spieron wasn't done, however.

Spieron pulled his phone out of his front pocket, where the top portion had been hanging out—that included the lens of the camera. While tapping the device to stop the recording, Spieron smiled at a dark-haired woman with a decidedly calculating air to her expression. He held up his device and asked, "Would you care for a video of the conversation you just witnessed?"

The brunette's eyes widened, then she smiled sweetly. "Why, yes please, handsome. That would be lovely."

After securing the woman's name—Regina—and her email address, Spieron swept his gaze over the rest of those assembled. "Would anyone else care for a copy?"

Only one other woman requested it. The rest seemed to be a bit too shocked to respond. Of course, there might have been someone there who considered the episode too vulgar to have a recording of.

Fortunately for Spieron and his plan, that didn't seem to be a prevailing feeling.

"I'll have this video to you shortly, ma'am," Spieron assured both guests. Then he turned back to face Albert. Seeing the blank expression on his beloved's pale face hurt Spieron more than any of Katrina's hateful words ever could have. Touching his lover's shoulder, Spieron murmured, "It's time to go, my beloved."

Albert sucked in a swift breath, then snapped his gaze to Spieron. After blinking once, his lover nodded. His smile appeared forced, but he began to turn.

"Of course." Albert paused an instant so he could tip his hat once more, saying, "Our apologies for the disruption, ladies. G'day."

Then Albert led the way back through the house. His back remained tense, and his fingers had a white-knuckled grip on his crutches. He hobbled more swiftly than Spieron had ever before seen him.

Even still, Albert managed to direct a tight smile Simon's way. The man had somehow pulled out of his own shocked stupor and had hustled to reach the front door before them. The butler held the door open, but his expression remained worried.

Albert paused in the doorway and met Simon's gaze. "If we caused you problems, please know we will do whatever we can to help you get another position." His smile finally began to relax a little as he added, "Or you could always return to the ranch." A teasing glint entered his eyes as he tipped his chin toward Simon and added, "Unless you like those monkey suits Katrina has started making you wear."

Simon's tension eased, and he even offered a soft chuckle. "Thank you, sir."

Spieron wasn't the only one who must have realized that was all the butler was going to say, for Albert began moving again, calling over his shoulder, "And tell Meredith good luck for me!"

"Yes, sir!"

Walking beside Albert, they made their way back to Spieron's truck in silence. He hit his key fob to unlock it, then opened the passenger door. After helping Albert into the cab, Spieron stowed the crutches in the back of the king cab.

By the time Spieron made it around to the other side, Albert had buckled himself in and unbuttoned the top few buttons of his shirt as well as the ones at his wrists.

"We have one more stop," Spieron murmured, rubbing

his beloved's thigh soothingly. "You still up for it?"

Albert inhaled deeply before letting it out slowly. Turning his head, he met Spieron's gaze. "Yes." His voice sounded a little strained, but his tone was firm. "Let's get this done."

Spieron nodded and released Albert. He slipped his truck's key into the ignition and fired up his vehicle. After clasping his own safety belt, Spieron put his truck into gear and pointed them in the direction of Vernon's law office.

CHAPTER TWELVE

"How does that feel?"

Albert peered down at his pale green cast. It went from just below his knee to his foot. Wiggling his toes, he slowly bent his knee. It felt stiff, but he sure was happy to no longer be in a full leg cast.

"Not bad," Albert replied, giving the dark-haired, female vampire a smile. "And I appreciate it even more that you flew in to take care of this."

Melissa laughed as she stood. "I'm happy to," she replied, resting her hands on her hips. Her green eyes gleamed as she offered him a saucy grin. "With all these hot cowboys around? Mmm-mmm-mmm." Waggling her brows, Melissa stated, "I'm on vacation."

Albert barked a laugh, amusement flooding him. After the stress of the last week, it felt damn good.

Things were still strained between Nicholas and Vernon—how could they not be—but at least Vernon had retracted the eviction notice. He'd also canceled the paperwork that was in the works to put the ranch in his name. There had been extra hurdles to jump through due to the fact that Baltus was in the hospital, so the paperwork hadn't been finalized.

Due to the video of Katrina's rant, where she'd admitted to fraud, which was somehow leaked onto the Internet, she and her assets were under investigation. Albert figured he would get who had done it right on the first guess. They had known it would happen, though, so when the investigation into Katrina and her assets had begun, they'd had all the necessary paperwork prepared to show that the ranch was to be passed to Nicholas should anything happen to Baltus.

Since Baltus was currently still in a coma with no sign yet of when he would wake, the paperwork to give Nicholas deed to the ranch had already begun. Vernon's paperwork had only paused it. Now, it was back on track again.

Albert had learned from Spieron that his lover had purposefully put Baltus's mind to sleep for at least three months. After that, he would wake confused, disoriented, and with excessive memory loss. The man would have to go through intensive physical therapy and schooling to relearn how to do things.

"Head injuries can be so unpredictable," the doctors would say.

"So, I'm sure you're curious if you're cleared for sex."

Melissa's bald statement yanked Albert out of his recollection of the happenings of the last few days. He felt blood rush to his cheeks as he stared wide-eyed at the slender vampire before him. Albert suddenly wished he still had his big, bushy beard, but he'd shaved most of the growth so he would look respectable while in town.

Fortunately, Spieron seemed to like his shorter whiskers. He constantly petted his jawline and rubbed his thumb over his upper lip. Hell, his vampire just seemed to love his body hair in general. Maybe it was because Spieron was nearly hairless.

"Oh, look at that vacant glaze to your eyes. You must be thinking about sex right now."

"Melissa!" Spieron barked.

The vampire doctor laughed, then headed toward the front living room's exit. "I'm going to stroll around the ranch." She giggled as she added, "See what fun I can find."

"Don't disrupt any of the men at work," Spieron ordered

gruffly.

Tossing her dark hair over her shoulder, Melissa quipped, "Would I do that?" Then she swept out the front door, disappearing from view.

"Yeah, I can see her causing trouble," Nicholas muttered as he entered the room right behind Spieron. Shaking his head, he settled on a recliner to Albert's right.

Spieron eased down to Albert's left on the sofa, then took his hand. "How are you feeling?"

"Okay," Albert replied.

"Sorry I had to steal him for a second," Nicholas cut in with a grimace. "We just might be getting another house guest for a while."

After slinging his arm around Spieron's waist so he could caress his opposite hip, Albert focused back on Nicholas. "What do you mean, son?"

"Vernon stopped by. We met him outside, since you were busy with the doc," Nicholas told him, rubbing his hand over his face. Meeting Albert's gaze, Nicholas admitted, "Vernon asked if he could stay here for a while . . . until the heat at his place in town dies off. Evidently, there are reporters staking out his home."

Albert hesitated just an instant, then asked, "Did you tell him yes?"

Nicholas nodded once. "He's my brother."

"Yes, he is," Albert replied immediately. He leaned to the side and squeezed Nicholas's knee before straightening. "He's family, and both his parents turned out to be assholes." Smirking, he rolled his eyes. "Hell, we ain't no prize, but I reckon we can at least show him what real loyalty is, eh?"

"Yeah, we can," Nicholas replied softly. His dark eyes softened, expressing his appreciation without words.

"Speaking of loyalty," Spieron cut in gruffly. "I think you

and I need to go and have a little talk."

Nicholas bounced from his chair, a wide grin on his face. "That's my cue to leave." Giving them both a cheeky smile, he told them, "The house will be empty for a few hours. Pauline is grocery shopping in town, and the rest of us are outside doing something or other. Have fun!" After crowing those final words, Nicholas rushed out the front door.

Albert couldn't remember the last time his cheeks had felt so damn hot. He scowled at Spieron. "Does everyone know we hoped to have sex after the cast was changed?"

Spieron chuckled huskily as he rose to his feet. Turning to face Albert, he held out his hand. "Is that really what you want to talk about." His vampire's green eyes gleamed as he grinned salaciously at him. "Or is there something else you'd like to discuss even more?"

From Spieron's sultry tenor as well as the look in his eyes, Albert felt his blood heat in his veins and swiftly flow south. Goose bumps broke out on his skin, and anticipation rushed through his body. His dick swelled in his jeans.

"Does it have anything to do with you claiming me and finishing our bond?" Albert responded gruffly as he slowly reached out and took Spieron's hand.

To Albert's pleasure, Spieron easily heaved him to his feet. His lover's hand on his hip steadied him, and he re-laxed into the man's support. After placing his hands on Spieron's shoulders, he slid them down his man's torso and rubbed over his lover's lean frame.

"Yes, it most definitely has everything to do with me claiming you and finishing our bond." Spieron's irises began to bleed red, betraying his excitement. "Tell me you're ready."

Seeing Spieron's need revealed in such an instinctual way caused a thrill to surge through Albert. "Oh, yes." His blood rushed through his veins, and he couldn't help but reach down and adjust his burgeoning erection. Albert pinned a hungry grin on Spieron before glancing down pointedly. "I'm definitely ready."

Spieron's nostrils flared, and a low moan escaped him. "Gods, I love seeing your response to me." He eased his grip and took a step backward, all the while making certain Albert maintained his balance. "Grab your crutches, my beloved." Licking his lips, Spieron growled low in his throat. "As tempted as I am to toss you over my shoulder like you did me that first time, I don't want to jostle your leg."

Albert's heart warmed for a whole new reason as he was carefully turned and urged to grab his crutches. His vampire was always looking out for him. Slipping them under his armpits, Albert began heading to their bedroom.

"Then you'd better follow, Spieron," Albert ordered. "I'm ready to finish what we started, for us to twine our life forces."

Spieron did as Albert ordered until they reached the bedroom door. Then his vampire slipped around him and opened said door, entering first. With his next move, he stripped, losing his clothes with a speed only a paranormal could attain.

As Albert closed the door, he admired the lean, powerful lines and smooth skin revealed to him. He sucked in a deep breath as his gaze landed on Spieron's erection. His lover was just as hard as he was, his long, hard prick extending from his thin thatch of reddish-brown curls. As Albert stared, a bead of pre-cum swelled from Spieron's slit.

When Spieron moaned, Albert snapped his focus back to his lover's face. His vampire's red-irised gaze stared right back at him. As Albert watched, Spieron licked his lips, then opened his mouth and ran the tip of his tongue down one fang, then up the other.

"Time to get you more comfortable," Spieron hissed,

stalking forward. "Drop the crutches and put your hands on my shoulders."

As soon as Albert obeyed, Spieron rested his hands on his hips. He lifted and pivoted, then with surprising care, placed him in the middle of the mattress. As Albert peered up at his needy lover, Spieron reached down and eased his shoe from his good foot.

Then Spieron made quick work of Albert's fly, allowing his hard shaft to jut between the flaps. Due to how often they went at it, Albert had taken to skipping underwear. It just got in the way.

Planting his left foot on the comforter, Albert pushed his hips up, helping his lover ease his jeans down. As soon as Spieron pulled them off his feet, he immediately crunched up and whipped his flannel shirt and t-shirt over his head. He tossed them aside, then sprawled on the mattress.

Albert took in Spieron's trembling frame, how his nostrils flared and his hands clenched and released. The need vibrating through his vampire, oh-so-carefully leashed yet barely contained, created a wave of answering desire to swell through him. While spreading his legs wider, Albert reached under the pillow on the left and grabbed the tube of lubricant they kept there.

"Take me, my vampire," Albert urged, holding up the tube. "I'm yours. I've been yours since the moment we met." Wiggling the tube, Albert growled low in his throat. "Make me feel you, Spieron."

Spieron growled, and the sound somehow seemed to vibrate in Albert's balls. His cock twitched, and goose bumps broke out on his thighs. When Spieron crawled between his knees, his red-eyed vampire popped the cap with one thumb.

"You wish me to make you feel me, beloved?" Spieron rasped, his hunger bleeding through in his voice.

Albert sucked in a harsh gasp even as he forced a nod. Seeing the feral gleam in Spieron's red eyes, a tremble worked through Albert. His cock twitched, and his body felt super-sensitive . . . which was only accentuated when Spieron teased his fingertips along the underside of his balls.

Groaning roughly, Albert shivered. His gut clenched and he watched with anticipation as Spieron poured plenty of fluid onto his fingers. When his vampire met his gaze and grinned, Albert felt his heart thud wildly as his pulse surged.

My vampire needs me.

After swallowing hard, Albert ordered, "Do it. You want to. I can see it in your eyes. Do what you want. I'm yours."

Spieron grinned widely, showing off his fangs. Then he leaned over Albert's groin, nuzzling his nose against Albert's balls. "Time to open you up, my sexy mountain man. Gonna relax you so fuckin' good."

"Yeah?" Albert panted harshly. "How ya gonna do that?"

"Like this."

Then Spieron lapped over Albert's balls, teasing the sensitive skin of his sack. At the same time, he rubbed his slicked fingertip over Albert's hole. As he suckled lightly at one nut, Spieron pushed his finger deep inside Albert's chute.

Albert clenched on instinct, but the way Spieron lapped and teased at his testicles nearly instantly eased him. His groin suddenly felt on fire. His thighs trembled, and his abdominals shuddered.

His erection twitched and throbbed. He felt his balls roll. The skin of his sack felt hyper-sensitive where Spieron rubbed his smooth chin over him.

"S-Spieron," Albert gasped, shocked to feel the tingle at the base of his spine. "I-I'm gonna—"

"Yes," Spieron growled. "Come for me."

Even if Albert had wanted to hold back, he couldn't. Right then, Spieron lifted away from his balls, opened his mouth, and sank down on his prick. When his vampire sucked upward, Albert couldn't stop it.

Moaning harshly, Albert shook as his orgasm washed through him. His seed pulsed from him in bliss-inducing spurts. Even the way Spieron rubbed his fingertips over his gland — *does he have two in me now* — made the sensations go on and on.

As soon as Albert stopped spurting, Spieron pulled off his prick. He immediately went back to lapping at his sack. Moaning upon feeling his lover gently play with his sensitized nerve endings, he shuddered and twitched.

Albert gasped, then hummed when he felt his vampire push another finger into his channel. His body felt stretched, but it felt amazing in a way he'd never before experienced. Panting softly, he rocked into each move of his lover's fingers.

"Oh, god!" Albert ground his teeth as his dick began to fill once more. "Now. Hurry the fuck up!"

Spieron met his gaze, a feral grin lighting his features. "Just one more thing."

Albert didn't even have a chance to ask.

In the next instant, Spieron opened his mouth and ever-so-gently sank his fangs part of the way into Albert's ball sack. Even before he could process the spike of pain, Spieron lapped around his embedded canines . . . then he sucked. When Albert's nerve endings registered the pain, the sensation was tempered by pleasure.

Then Spieron wrapped his lips around his testicles and sucked.

Albert bellowed as the most exquisite mixture of bliss and pain swept through his system. His cock unloaded again, and his body shook and trembled. Sweat broke out on his skin as he kept coming and coming.

Panting harshly, his senses singing, Albert barely registered it when Spieron released his testicles. He watched le-thargically, knowing his smile was probably bliss-drunk. His vampire didn't seem to care as he crawled over Albert and levered over his body.

"Albert, my beloved." Spieron took Albert's mouth in a possessive kiss for several seconds, then broke it and gave him a feral smile. "Now, you are *mine*."

Before Albert had to think up a response, he felt Spieron's cock sink into his body. As his muscles gave way, his re-laxed state created by the double orgasm meant he barely felt a hint of pain. The slide of Spieron's cock over his pros-tate drew a moan from his lips.

"That's a sound I love hearing from your lips," Spieron stated, his voice raspy.

When Albert wrapped his arms around Spieron, gripping his lover, he grinned up at him. "I like making it."

Albert would have blushed at his cheesy line, but Spieron immediately responded with, "Then I'll make you do it often."

In the next instant, Albert's brain shut down as Spieron delivered on his promise. As he floated away on the endor-phins created by multiple orgasms, he realized that he and his lover just might set a new record that day . . . and he couldn't wait to enjoy every second of the experience.

Love you, Albert thought.

In Albert's mind, he felt certain he received a response.

Love you, too, my beloved mountain man.

"How's the data mining of Krakow's files going?"

Growling low in his throat, Vincentius admitted, "Not as well as I'd hoped. He either hid his tech-savvy abilities, or he has someone in his employ that is damn good." Turning toward the doors, he fell into step with Aiden as he began walking. "I've been hitting so many dead ends and finding so many false trails, it's ridiculous."

"Damn, I'm sorry to hear that."

Vincentius shrugged. Since all shifter files had to be routed through hidden databases on the darknet to keep them out of the hands of unsuspecting humans, it was no wonder the answers were difficult to find. Those who set up such things were normally fantastic hackers in their own right.

"I just need to figure out who in Krakow's employ is doing this, then figure out their signature. Every hacker has one." Seeing the uncomprehending look on Aiden's face even as he nodded, Vincentius bit back a chuckle. He could get a little carried away talking about his passion. "I'll keep working on it. At least with Councilman Alvaro here, I have access to every single report the Stone Ridge wolves sent us. I can use them to work backward."

"Awesome. Glad to hear it." Aiden gripped his shoulder, the blond deer shifter smiling at him. "I heard Councilman Alvaro is big into poker. He and his wife are putting together a meet and greet poker night on Saturday. Are you going?"

Vincentius nodded. "I am." He'd never played poker with any of the councilmen. In fact, he couldn't recall doing anything recreational with them. "It should be . . . interesting."

Told ya Shane would shake up our boring asses.

He mentally laughed at himself.

Aiden chuckled quietly. "Yeah. That's a good way to put it." Coming to a T-junction, the other man waved and turned toward the left. "See you later."

Vincentius waved and headed toward the right, toward the parking garage and home. He was flanked by the council enforcer assigned to him while within the council building's walls. Each councilman had one, and normally they were considered a friend. His was Tideus Solverman, a big saltwater crocodile shifter. His personal guard and best friend — Seever Kerns, a fellow lion shifter who he'd grown up with, also handled Vincentius's home security. Hell, the man practically ran his household. Seever had fallen into step, flanking him, after leaving the central chamber.

After Vincentius glanced over his shoulder at each man, he asked, "What about you guys? You poker players? You wanna go?" He recalled Seever playing a hand or two, but it'd always been Vincentius's idea. Tideus had been assigned to his detail only two years before, and he still didn't know much about the thick-bodied, powerful male. If neither man wanted the interaction, Vincentius knew he could count on them to find someone who would want to go while still being able to do their jobs.

"If you're offering, I'm going," Tideus replied, grinning

widely. "I'll show you all how it's done."

Seever scoffed. "You wish. I'll whoop your ass."

Grinning, he felt pleased that he would have men there that he considered friends.

More than ready to go home so he could get to his nap, Vincentius climbed into the back of the SUV, then leaned his bucket seat all the way back, trusting Seever to drive him home.

His phone beeping penetrated Vincentius's dreams. He groaned as he rolled over and grabbed the device. As soon as he managed to crack open an eyelid and read the alert, he jolted to a sitting position.

All vestiges of sleep disappeared as adrenaline flooded his body.

"Holy fucking shit," Vincentius hissed as he shot from the bed. He just remembered to yank on a pair of cut-off sweats before he barreled out of his room naked. While it wouldn't have been the first time, he attempted to curb the habit during daylight hours. Once his genitals were covered, Vincentius stalked through the house, grumbling under his breath. "Who the hell would hack me?"

Vincentius couldn't remember the last time that had happened.

Settling behind his computer, Vincentius watched as lines of code appeared on his screen. He scowled as he read the person's intent.

Damn. The guy ain't subtle. He has all the finesse of a steamroller.

After a moment of watching where the hacker was going and what he was accessing, Vincentius lifted his hands to the keyboard and began carefully doing a back-hack, tracing the unknown user's steps, so he could figure out who it could be and where they were located.

Hours later, Vincentius stared at the screen in shock. The

hack had originated near Stone Ridge, Colorado . . . and the user was not listed as a wolf shifter. Could Shane have unknown intentions, after all? Was he planning to harm the Shifter Council and place Alpha Declan McIntire as the king of all shifters, just as Paraben Krakow claimed?

While the idea seemed ludicrous, Vincentius had to find out for certain. He crossed to his office's intercom and hit the button that would open a line to his security office. "Seever?"

"It's Willow, sir." A female voice came through the line. "Master Kerns went off at seven."

Glancing at a nearby monitor, Vincentius winced. It was almost eleven at night. Slept longer than I thought. "Right, well . . . I need you to track down Investigator Nkosi Akintola. I need him here asap."

Vincentius heard Willow hiss as she inhaled sharply. Still, an instant later, she replied, "Y-Yes, sir. As soon as I track him down, I'll contact you."

"Thank you."

Vincentius released the button and turned back to his screen. Patience wasn't his strong suit, but he knew he had no choice. For this sort of delicate retrieval, he needed the best, and that was Nkosi.

The black mamba shifter would be able to infiltrate Stone Ridge.

About the Author

Charlie started writing fantasy when she was eight, and after stumbling onto her first erotic romance at age nineteen, she realized her true calling. She now focuses on writing gay erotic romance, normally of the paranormal variety, with heroes of all kinds. With the help and support of her husband, Charlie finally fulfilled one of her life-long goals . . . move to acreage with her horses. You can often find her curled up with her laptop and a cup of tea or glass of wine, creating her next adventure. Charlie enjoys exploring the mountains of her new Oregon home on horseback, 4-wheeler, or motorcycle.

She can be reached at ch.richards2010@yahoo.com
Or visit her at www.charlie-richards.com